ON THE LINE

DUBLIN NIGHTS

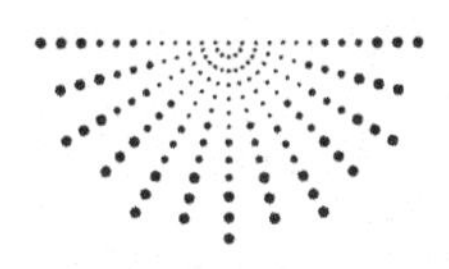

BRITTNEY SAHIN

EMKO MEDIA

On the Line: A Dublin Nights Novella

By: Brittney Sahin

Published by: EmKo Media, LLC

Copyright © 2019 EmKo Media, LLC

This book is an original publication of Brittney Sahin.

In accordance with the U.S. Copyright Act of 1976, the scanning, uploading, and electronic sharing of any part of this book without permission of the publisher constitute unlawful piracy and theft of the author's intellectual property. If you would like to use material from the book (other than for review purposes), prior written permission must be obtained by contacting EmKoMedia@gmail.com. Thank you for your support of the author's rights.

Editor: Anja, HourGlass Editing

Proofreader: Judy Zweifel, Judy's Proofreading

Cover Design: LJ, Mayhem Cover Creations

Image: Shutterstock

This book is a work of fiction. Names, characters, places, and incidents either are products of the author's imagination or are used fictitiously. Any resemblance to actual persons, living or dead, business establishments, events, or locales is entirely coincidental.

Ebook ISBN: 9781947717169

Paperback ISBN: 9781797557755

Created with Vellum

To Nancy and Arielle - I couldn't have written this without you. Thank you!

CHAPTER ONE

ADAM

"I KNOW IT'S BAD LUCK TO SEE THE BRIDE ON HER WEDDING day, but is it bad luck to talk?" My hands landed on each side of the doorframe as I waited for a response. My heartbeat rose with every silent second.

No way was she having second thoughts.

"Please, Anna, can you just tell me to bugger off, at least? I need to hear your voice to know you're okay." I shook the door handle as if that'd do something.

"Still nothing?" my sister, Holly, asked.

I turned to see Anna's sisters trailing behind Holly.

The looks they were giving me as they neared . . . sympathy. Like they assumed Anna had pulled a runaway bride move.

"You think something's wrong?" Dana, Anna's younger sister, stopped in front of me. "When she didn't answer I got worried."

"You did the right thing in getting me." I grabbed my mobile from my pocket. "This is Adam McGregor. I need someone to open the honeymoon suite," I said straight away when the hotel front desk picked up. "Bring a key. Now."

Silence spanned the line for the space of a heartbeat, like the woman was questioning whether Anna had taken off as well. "Be right there."

"There's something wrong." I could feel it in my gut.

"I'm sure there's an innocent explanation as to why she's not answering." Holly was attempting to be the voice of reason, the calm in the ever-growing storm.

I cradled the back of my neck and tipped my gaze skyward on the verge of losing my bloody mind.

Be okay. Please, be okay.

"When was the last time you saw her?" I glimpsed a look at Anna's older sister, Becca, cutting a path between Holly and Dana to get to me.

Every memory from last night snapped through my mind as I waited for Becca to answer.

"I saw her around midnight before I went to bed. And then when I knocked on her door this morning there was no answer," Becca replied.

"Same," Dana said.

"We thought she was in the shower," Becca added. "We waited for enough time to pass before coming to get you when she still didn't answer."

Feck. I redialed her number, then lowered the mobile to my side and pressed my ear to the door, trying to listen for a ring.

"Anything?" Holly placed a hand on my forearm, and I shook my head and ended the call.

"Mr. McGregor." I pivoted to find a woman heading our way. "Everything okay?"

"That's what I'm trying to find out." My throat tightened.

"Hopefully she didn't slip in the shower or something," Dana said.

An idea I hadn't thought of. "Can you hurry and open the damn door?"

"But it'll be bad luck to see—"

"Just open the door," I hissed at the woman through barely parted teeth, ready to pummel my way through the door to get to Anna.

She sidestepped me to open it.

"Anna!" I flung the door open so hard it hit the wall and came back at me, so I blasted it out of my way again. "Anna?"

The bedroom. Closet. Shower. All empty.

"She's not here." I hung my head, searching for breath.

I redialed Anna's number, and my eyes connected with Holly's as I waited and hoped she'd pick up. To tell me she was grabbing a snack downstairs.

But . . .

I turned my head at the faint sound of a ringtone. I followed the noise and crouched to the side of the bed.

"Her phone." Dana pressed a hand over her mouth at the sight of Anna's mobile in my grasp. "She wouldn't run without—" She dropped her words when her eyes whipped to my face.

Heat licked beneath my skin like a fire ready to eviscerate everything down to my last breath.

I killed the call and tucked my mobile into my pocket, then entered the four-digit code to Anna's mobile and scrolled through her last calls then texts.

Nothing abnormal.

"Do you have security cameras on these floors?" I asked the woman since there was nothing unusual on Anna's phone. And hell, nothing unusual about the room.

No signs of a struggle.

The woman blinked. "I . . . Yes, we do."

"I need to see them." I rubbed at my forehead, trying to collect my racing thoughts, and then I left the room.

"Adam." Holly followed me. "What do you want me to do?"

I faced her once outside the lift. "Look for her in the hotel. Don't tell anyone anything until we know what's going on."

"I'm sure she's still here, and we're all overreacting." She was trying to reassure me, but that was impossible.

"She wouldn't risk bumping into me on the day of our wedding by wandering the hotel. She's too nervous about everything." The lift doors parted, and we headed inside. "But look anyway."

I clutched my chest while we descended, as I grappled with possibilities.

Anna had either run away—or . . . she was taken.

Either way, it felt like the end of the fecking world.

* * *

"DID YOUR BRIDE-TO-BE RUN?" A REPORTER HOLLERED AS I surged through the crowd with my brothers on each side of me acting as bodyguards.

The press continued to huddle around us as we pushed through them.

The cameras snapping pictures. The lights. The questions. I shielded my eyes as if the sun were in my face as I moved.

"What enemies do you have?" someone asked.

"Who may have taken her?" another voice ripped through the air.

"Get them out of here!" my twin brother, Sean, yelled to the two hotel guards who were failing miserably to gain control of the situation.

"What'd you do to make her leave?" a woman asked, and I caught sight of my younger brother, Ethan, halt in place.

"How about you go to hell?" Ethan sputtered, then looked at me and tipped his chin toward the lift, motioning for me to get out of there.

"Why are you letting these people in here?" I heard Sean's question roar from behind as I closed in on the lift.

I couldn't bring myself to look back, to see the throngs of people eyeing me as if Anna's disappearance was my fault.

Once inside the lift, I bowed my head.

I had to keep it together.

She wouldn't run; I knew it. She'd been worried something would jinx the wedding. No way would she leave me.

But the idea that someone took her was like scorpions crawling across my flesh, stinging my skin in every place at once.

"No one came in or out," the detective in charge said the second I met him inside my hotel suite.

I'd called the Garda, the police in Dublin, and reported her missing. And if I wasn't a McGregor, they would've told me to wait forty-eight hours before filing a report. Hell, they probably would've told me she ran away and didn't want to marry me.

But . . . because of my money, my last name—half the officers in Dublin now flooded the hotel. The unfortunate side effect: reporters barking out questions and accusations.

My parents were handling the guests for me, letting them know Anna was gone and attempting to field their questions.

I wasn't ready to face any of them. I could barely look at myself in the mirror—let alone anyone else.

"McGregor?"

I blinked at the sound of my name coming from the

detective's mouth. "Yeah?" My eyes were blurry. My vision obstructed by unshed tears. I couldn't fight the battle of emotions ripping through me, shredding me into scraps of nothing.

"The cameras show your fiancée entering her room at midnight last night, so unless she learned how to fly and went out the window, someone must've tampered with the security footage."

His words had my gaze swinging to his face, and my heartbeat climbed higher and higher.

"Any enemies you may have? Someone who may have taken her?"

He halted his line of questioning so I could collect my thoughts. Not exactly possible, though. My thoughts were scattered all over the place.

"Enemies . . . I . . . the only guy who'd want to hurt me like this is already dead," I said slowly.

"Donovan Hannigan?"

"Yeah." Donovan had been the Dublin crime boss who'd sunk his teeth into me when I was a teenager, creating the fighter I'd become.

But Donovan's body had washed up in a river five kilometers south of the city less than three months ago—shortly after Da's heart attack. There wasn't much left of Donovan's face, but I'd insisted on seeing him to confirm he was no longer a threat to Anna or my family.

It'd been him, though. The bastard was dead.

"Donovan could have family who may want revenge. We'll look into it." Detective Grady, I think that was his name, took a breath. A long-winded one. "Anyone else? Your family runs a multibillion-dollar empire, surely, you've acquired enemies? Ever receive threats? Hate mail?"

I held my palms in the air. "Not that I'm aware of." I

couldn't imagine who'd target my family. Well, *me*. They took Anna, so this had to be an attack against me.

The man stroked his brown beard before his hands slipped into his pockets. "If not enemies, then maybe someone saw this as an opportunity to score a high-priced ransom."

"How often do you see the person safely returned when ransoms are paid?"

He was quiet for a bit. "About half the time."

A fifty percent chance.

No, those odds weren't good enough.

"Adam?" I looked to see Marco Valenti entering the hotel room. We'd become friends since he was on the football team my family owned in Rome. "Can I talk to you for a second?" He motioned for me to step out into the hall.

He was probably going to offer condolences of some sort —but that was the last thing I wanted, which was why I'd stayed away from as many wedding guests as possible since I'd discovered she was gone.

All I wanted was Anna back safe in my arms.

"Give me a second." I crossed the room and went out into the hall with him.

"Hey." A tight line cut across Marco's forehead as he observed me. Pain in his eyes. An echo of my own.

I bit down on my back teeth as I waited for his words, for an apology to flow between us—for the moment I'd want to knock the word *sorry* away.

"Maggie wanted to come, but I, uh, figured you'd, eh, need space." His Italian accent whipped through his tone harder than normal.

Good call.

"I know the police are here, but my buddy's wife . . . well, finding and helping people is her sister's expertise," he said in a low voice, catching me off guard, and I leaned in closer to try and absorb what he was saying. "She was MI6. I'm not supposed to know, but she works freelance with a new team."

I looked to the floor, my head spinning.

"I made a call, and they're catching a flight out of London to come here. I'm sorry, but I didn't know what to do for you and—"

"Thank you." I found his eyes again. "I'll take all the help I can get."

He braced a hand on my shoulder, and emotions settled in the back of my throat. That or it was the rise of bile, and I was ready to lose my dinner from last night all over Marco's shoes.

"I'll let you know when they get here." Marco nodded.

"Thanks," I think I said as I caught sight of my brothers heading my way.

"Anything?" Sean asked once Marco left.

My twin brother and I looked nothing alike, and we couldn't be more different in every single way, but somehow, he'd always been able to feel my pain. Channel it. And the way he was looking at me right now was as if he lost his fiancée, too.

"Looks like someone tampered with the cameras." I rubbed at my forehead, collecting my thoughts.

"So, she didn't run." Ethan's words had my hand falling to my side as I observed him.

"No," I said through gritted teeth.

"I'm sorry. It would've been a better alternative to . . . you know." Ethan shoved his hands into his trouser pockets. "Sorry."

I dropped my gaze to the floor.

My mind was going blank. My body numb.

"I'm going to take a drive. Look around the city. I don't

know. I want to do something," Sean said. "You want to come with me?"

I knew he was directing his question at Ethan because as much as I wanted to go search for her, combing the streets would be a waste of time. But if it made my brother feel better, or even useful, I wouldn't stop him.

"Yeah," Ethan said. "We'll check in."

"Call us if you hear anything." Sean gripped my shoulder and found my eyes. "We're going to get her back."

I gulped, trying to hide my emotions. No fecking luck. "Yeah, of course we will," I said, willing my words to be true.

I went back into the room after my brothers left, and my gaze wandered to Anna's parents. My future father-in-law, who officially hated me almost as much as I now hated myself, clutched his wife in a tight embrace.

His eyes swept to mine and thinned.

I'd never felt like such a failure in all my life.

I had to get Anna back.

And I'd lay everything on the line to do it.

CHAPTER TWO

ANNA

EIGHT DAYS EARLIER

"It really is amazing." And yet, a tremble in my hands had me clutching the second-floor railing even tighter as I observed the two-story wall of windows. The evening sun spilled into the room as the fiery ball began its descent.

The expansive living room down below was decorated more beautifully than I'd ever envisioned when Adam and I had sat down with the designer six months ago. A mix of country from my Southern roots with splashes of modernity to go with Adam's style.

"Are you sure we're not jinxing anything if we move in before we're married, though?" I couldn't help but ask.

Adam's hands wrapped around my waist from behind, and my nervous energy began to dissipate. The man was an expert at calming me, but he could also ignite my desires from zero to sixty within the space of a heartbeat.

Jury was out on which I wanted at the moment. Maybe both.

"If you want to wait until after the wedding we can."

Sandalwood and a hint of pine touched my nose as I shifted my face over my shoulder and inhaled his intoxicating scent.

His mouth brushed against mine.

"Kiss me like that again, and we'll be making love instead of heading out." I pivoted to fully face him and looped my arms around his neck.

"Promise?" His blue eyes glinted with the sunlight catching his irises. "Why don't we skip the parties and stay in?"

"Mm." I nipped his bottom lip and felt his cock harden against me. "As much as I'd love to feel you inside of me, we have to wait. Plus, I don't want to suffer the wrath of my bridesmaids. This would be the second time I canceled the bachelorette party."

"First time wasn't your fault." He shifted back a touch to find my eyes, and I could see a hint of worry there. Maybe his nerves were as tangled as mine.

"What does the bridal party have planned tonight, anyway?" He arched a brow.

"No idea. Your sister is like Fort Knox, and Becca—well, you've met her. She's as tight-lipped as they come." I squinted one eye and studied him. "But you already questioned them, didn't you?" My fingers skated to the knot of his tie, and I adjusted it.

"Can you blame me, love?" His hands shifted to my ass, and he squeezed. "They wouldn't tell me anything, but the idea of some guy stripping for you . . ." He dropped his words and shook his head. "Let's just say I'm gonna have a bloody stroke thinking about you out in the city unprotected tonight."

"And you'll be with the guys. I'm sure your brothers and Les are up to a whole lot of no good."

"Not if I can help it." He pressed a quick kiss to my lips.

"I have everything I need right here." He lost his hold of me and stepped back to view my abdomen. "Well, almost everything."

A baby. As soon as we tied the knot we'd begin trying.

"Let's stay in. I don't even want to know what kind of shenanigans Les and my brothers have planned for me. And as for you," he said while grabbing my hand and pulling me tight against him, "I think we could jumpstart our plans. Make love in every room. I can come inside of you."

"Mm. But making you wait until the wedding night is way too much fun."

"For you, maybe. But my balls are about to fall off." His forehead touched mine.

"It's only been a week," I said with a chuckle.

"That's like four eternities." He groaned and rotated his hips so his shaft pressed against me.

I stepped back and out of his reach, and his arms swooped to his sides. My gaze journeyed south to his belt buckle as my tongue raced over my bottom lip.

Part of me wanted to break my own rules.

To strip.

To have my soon-to-be husband take me right then and there.

But as painful as the waiting would be, the anticipation would add more fireworks to our already crazy-amazing sex life.

"Woman." A partial grunt left his lips as he reached for me and scooped me into his arms.

"Put me down," I said, but hooked my hands around his neck as he carried me to our new master bedroom. "Don't even think about it."

He tossed me onto the four-poster bed, climbed on top of me, and pinned me beneath him. "We'll wait," he said as he lowered his mouth close to mine. "But it's only fair I get to tease you since you've been killing me all week."

"What? Walking around naked in my cowboy boots last night bothered you?" I bit my lip.

"Just a wee bit, yeah." He kept his one hand near my shoulder on the bed, holding the brunt of his weight, and his other popped the buttons of my blouse open. He shoved my demi-bra down to free my breasts.

It was me groaning this time when he squeezed my flesh and lightly pinched my nipple. Heat pooled in my stomach and dipped lower, and I tightened my thighs, hoping to contain the desire flashing through me. I wanted to spread my legs and have him thrust inside of me like never before.

"Adam," I said with a pout when his hand settled between my legs, and he began strumming his fingers there. "This feels so good, but . . . I'm not giving in." My eyes squeezed closed as everything inside of me nearly burst.

I was already close to climaxing.

"Maybe this was a mistake. Now I'm more turned on than ever." He dropped next to me and reached down to cover his erection. "Am I allowed to jerk off, at least?" He rolled to his side to face me, but his gaze dipped to my breasts still on display.

"Hm. I guess that doesn't violate our no-sex-until-the-wedding deal."

He stood and cracked his neck. "Then you know what I'll be doing when I'm showering before I go out tonight."

"Thinking about me while I'm thinking about you during my shower?" I hopped off the bed and fixed my blouse as he attempted to adjust his pants, fighting his arousal.

"Eight more days," he said under his breath. "Eight more bloody days."

I extended my palm to shake his hand. "So, we agree not

to come back here until after we say *I do*?" When he clasped his hand with mine he yanked me to him and brought both his palms to my face.

"I love you so damn much." Emotion caught in his throat as he spoke. "And next weekend you're going to be my wife." His blue eyes pinned me still. "My wife," he whisper-said as if it were truly hitting him.

"You sure you don't want to skip all the pomp and circumstance and say *I do* in front of a few people, and then just ride off on some horses into the sunset?"

I wasn't totally kidding. I'd never been a big fan of being in the spotlight. It was probably why it took me forever to set the date and plan the wedding. The idea of having hundreds of eyes on me had my stomach doing somersaults.

Falling in the super-duper high heels my younger sister, Dana, had pressured me into buying? Probably.

Bawl my eyes out during the vows and have my waterproof mascara fail to come through for me? More than likely.

But . . . I'd do anything for this man. Luxurious wedding and all.

"You deserve the world. You deserve everything." He kissed me hard. "And I'm going to spend my life making sure you're happy."

"Mm. Well, goal achieved. I already am."

CHAPTER THREE

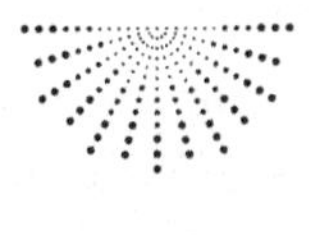

ANNA

"OKAY. I HAVE TO KNOW. WHO PICKED THIS PLACE?" I surveyed the members of my bachelorette party, trying to figure out who'd choose such a ridiculously lavish nightclub.

Becca, my oldest sister—no way in hell.

My youngest sister, Dana—maybe.

My other sister Sheri—that'd be a hard no.

My best friend, Lana, from back home who spends more time with horses than people? Highly doubt it.

No way would Holly McGregor pick a club with electronic dance music pulsing so loud you could barely hear yourself think. Plus, I'd caught her on her work phone only every other minute since our night began. The woman couldn't let loose.

"Kate?" I eyed my friend, and she coyly smiled and raised her hand.

"Guilty," she said. "It was suggested to me by this hottie with a megawatt smile."

Of course. "You spot him yet?"

She shook her head. "But tonight's not about me, anyway." She winked.

Kate and I had competed for an internship when I first came to Dublin—neither of us landing the role, but we'd stayed friends, and I was honored she'd flown in from New York for the party and the wedding. Especially for the second time.

"I tried to stop her from switching the location, but you know Kate," Narisa said.

Narisa did, in fact, win the internship with McGregor Enterprises, making the official move from Thailand to Dublin, which worked out since she'd fallen in love with Rick, one of the other interns who'd won.

"Well, I guess I can handle this." A wild nightclub bursting from the seams with drunken people wasn't exactly my go-to for a Friday night. But at least there were no dildo-shaped balloon hats to wear.

Our matching bridal tees were the only sign we were partaking in the time-honored tradition of a bachelorette party. Of course, my breasts were spilling out of the top, thanks to Dana, who I was pretty sure got the sizes purposefully wrong when she'd ordered our tees.

"Yeah, this wouldn't have been my first pick." Holly looked up from her phone. "Considering the devil owns this place." She averted her gaze to the second floor of the three-tiered club, and I followed her eyes to a man in an all-black suit with his forearms resting over the railing, his eyes pointed toward us.

He didn't even bother looking away when I caught him staring. "He's the owner?" A chill traveled down my spine, so I ripped my focus away from him.

"Yeah," Holly answered and looked back at me. "Sebastian Renaud."

"Is he a criminal?" Memories from my experiences with the Dublin crime boss, Donovan Hannigan, raced to mind.

The last thing I needed was to be in some sketchy place. I wanted to make it to my wedding day alive after all.

"No, nothing illegal. Well, I don't think. But he's known for making deals. And frankly, I don't like him. Half French. Half Irish. And a whole lot of douche." Holly's eyes went right back to her phone.

"Okay. No more phones!" Kate snatched her cell and held it above her head, and I was fairly certain Holly's eyes were going to pop.

Kate was the only one ballsy enough to do such a thing.

Even though my relationship with Holly had grown leaps and bounds since my engagement with Adam, the woman was still fairly emotionally closed off. All work. No play.

"I'm trying to save our media business from a . . ." Holly's words disappeared into the air. She stood and tried to snatch the phone from Kate, but Kate tossed it to Becca.

My poor sister had no interest in playing hot potato with a billionaire tigress, so she handed it back to Holly.

Standing with my hands on my hips—only one drink in me from the limo ride over—I squinted at Holly. Not the best idea since the room flashed with blinking lights, making it already hard to see. "What's up? Something wrong?"

"Forget I said anything." And yet, a hiss left her barely parted lips, and she returned her focus to her phone to type again.

"You sure you don't want to talk about it?" I asked.

"No." When she finished typing, she looked at me and frowned. "Shit. This is your night, and I suck at all of this. Sorry, love."

"Which is why I had to step in and help plan." Kate flashed her white teeth. "Thank God for me, or we'd have ended up at a bar with a bunch of uptight men in suits."

I laughed. “Good point,” I said when noticing a server heading our way with a tray of champagne and Grey Goose.

“Let the party begin!” Kate rubbed her palms together and motioned for us to sit.

The server poured eight shots of vodka, and my stomach protested at the sight. But what the hell—it was my bachelorette party. And I was about to become Mrs. McGregor. It was time to celebrate.

We clinked our little glasses together, and I winced after swallowing the clear liquid.

My sister coughed, sputtering some of the vodka out of her mouth. I forgot Dana was only twenty. The drinking age in Ireland was different than in Kentucky, but I didn’t want her to spend all of tomorrow hugging the toilet.

“Easy,” I said as non-motherly as possible.

“The second will go down smoother.” Narisa winked at Dana and began pouring another round.

“Thank God we ate a ton of greasy food before we got here,” Becca said with a laugh. “At my bachelorette party we sipped Chardonnay. This is—”

“Perfect!” Kate interjected. “Now, cheers to the bride-to-be. May you be fruitful and prosper.” She swiped a hand through the air. “Or something like that.”

All eyes expectantly went to Holly to see if she’d say anything.

Holly smoothed a hand down her shirt as if to collect her thoughts first. “You turned my brother’s life around,” she said. “And I’ve never seen him so happy. Thank you. I can’t wait to have a sister.” Her words had my heart squeezing in my chest. “Sláinte.”

My cheeks hurt from smiling. “Sláinte,” I repeated before taking the next shot.

After one more shot and a flute of champagne, we found

ourselves on the dance floor. The hard-hitting beat of the drums and bass from the music pulsed through me, and my skin tingled from the warmth of the alcohol.

I lost track of time or how many more drinks I'd had after that. The room hadn't started to spin yet, so that was a plus.

"Getting water. Be back!" I yelled over the music so my group could hear and then moved through the crowd of women and men throwing their hands in the air like they were at a rave.

"What can I get you?" The bartender placed a napkin on the counter, and his green eyes glowed from the flashing lights reflecting off his irises.

"Just water. Thank you."

His gaze dipped to the letters on my shirt. "Getting married, are ya?"

"A week from tomorrow," I answered a little breathlessly and averted my eyes over my shoulder to the dance floor.

Kate was grinding up against some random guy, and not to my surprise, Holly was waving away a young Brad Pitt lookalike. It'd take a hell of a lot to win Holly over.

"On the house."

I looked back at the bartender and found the bottle of water. "Thank you."

"She needs something a wee bit stronger, don't you think?" a man off to my left asked.

"I'm good. Thanks." I started to leave, but his hand curved around my bicep.

"You sure, love?" His eyes thinned as he observed me. And maybe it was the alcohol, but the man reminded me a little of my ex. An asshole, at best. And this guy was the last thing I wanted to deal with on a night like this.

"You can take your hand off me now." Adam had taught

me self-defense, but I wasn't itching to use my moves on the night of my party.

"How about a dance first?" His brows drew inward, and I wondered if the bartender would intervene, but when I glanced over at him he was busy helping someone else.

"How about you let me go, or I make you?" I plastered on a fake smile and cocked my head. The son of a bitch had less than five seconds to back down.

Gone was the meek and defenseless girl I'd been in Kentucky. I'd become a different woman since moving to Dublin. A stronger woman.

A real man, like Adam, always builds a woman up and never tears her down.

And I was so grateful for him.

"Don't you want one last fling before you get hitched?" His lips depressed into a hard line, and an unsettling feeling curled into a tight ball in my stomach.

"Back the feck off, and get the hell out of my club."

The man released his hold and hesitantly left, and I pivoted to find Sebastian Renaud. After what Holly had said about him, he was a man I had a feeling I didn't want to be indebted to.

"Thanks. I was handling it, though." I grabbed my water from the counter, almost forgetting why I'd come to the bar in the first place, and escaped back into the thick of the crowd, not interested in engaging in a conversation with the man. There was something haunting in his dark-brown eyes.

Holly pulled me off to the side of the dance floor and away from the DJ booth. "Hey, what did Renaud want with you? I was about to come kick his arse when I saw him talking to you."

Maybe Holly was more like Adam than she realized?

"He was saving me from a jerk."

Her mouth rounded in surprise. "Oh. Er, okay." She turned, probably expecting me to follow her back, but at the feel of someone's hand on my hip a moment later I remained frozen in place.

My head bowed.

Call me crazy, but the way I felt whenever Adam touched me was unmistakable.

"Hi, my love," he said into my ear, his warm breath sending spine-tingling sensations down my body.

"Mm. What are you doing here?" I allowed him to support some of my weight as he embraced me, pinning my back to his chest.

"Well, after two failed attempts before this place—Sean suggested it," he said loud enough for me to hear over a song I recognized by DJ Snake and Bieber—*Let Me Love You.*

I moved my ass and hips against him to the beat, and then he spun me around and lifted my arms up to drape over his shoulders.

His eyes greeted mine when his hands settled on my hips. He stared at me so deeply it was as if his soul could latch with mine somehow, like our togetherness could transcend space and time.

I leaned into him, but when I caught sight of the guy who'd hit on me watching me from across the room, I flinched and staggered back.

Did the guy actually think I'd chosen to cheat tonight—just not with him?

My stomach turned.

"Something wrong?" Adam's eyes thinned, and his lips became a white slash as the flashing lights flickered across his face, tinting him in an orange and green hue.

"I, uh." I looked to the floor, gathering my thoughts. If I told Adam about the jackass who'd hit on me, he might slug the guy, and that was the last thing I wanted right before our wedding.

No, I couldn't chance it.

"My head is starting to spin from the drinks." Not a lie. The effects of the alcohol were beginning to impact my balance.

"You want to sit? Go?"

"Why are you guys here?" Kate asked from behind before I could answer.

My shoulders slumped at being caught with him, something I knew she wouldn't let me live down.

"No boys allowed during our party," Kate said. "This is against the rules."

I pulled away from Adam to view her crossed arms and the pout on her face.

"This wasn't intentional," Adam said and stood alongside me. "But what'd you expect me to do when I saw Anna?"

Kate was looking at someone, or something else now, and so I turned to track her gaze.

Sean, Ethan, and Les were at the bar ordering drinks. Oblivious to our presence.

As much as his best friend, Les, drove me nuts, he'd been the one to bring Adam and me together.

If Les hadn't once rented his flat to me under his given name, Leslie, my life in Dublin could've turned out very differently.

From the moment I'd laid eyes on Adam I'd been hooked. Head over heels. Insta-lust that had grown into a forever-kind-of-love I'd once only thought existed in Disney movies or between the pages of books.

"You should go," Kate told him, and her words had me focusing back on her.

"No. Stay," I found myself saying.

"Anna." The plea in Kate's voice gave me pause.

"Give me a minute, okay?"

She eyed Adam before her gaze swept over to the bachelor party continuing without the groom-to-be. "Fine."

"Damn," Adam said with a smirk after she left. "She's tough."

"Yeah, remind me not to plan her party whenever she ties the knot. I'd massively fail, I'm sure."

He took my hand and led me to a booth hidden from our friends and siblings.

Once we were seated, he leaned back against the dark leather. "I don't miss this life."

"The wild nights you had before you met me?"

"My nights are pretty wild now if you ask me." He lightly shrugged. "Well, not since you've withheld sex this week, but normally, they're off the charts."

I blushed as if others could hear his words, even though no one was within earshot. "Next weekend can't come soon enough."

"Tell me about it."

"So . . ." I smiled. "Where'd you end up going before here?" I couldn't help but wonder, especially since he'd brought it up.

He shook his head. "Les brought me to some new fight club."

Les—of course. I should've known. "What was he thinking?"

He held his palms in the air. "He thought I'd enjoy throwing down with some young blood. You should've seen Sean when we got there. He pretty much body-slammed Les, then nearly got his arse whooped by him. My brother really needs to learn how to fight."

"Um." I blinked a few times. "Les does know we're

getting married? Bruises in wedding photos don't usually look all that great."

"Like I'd get bruised?"

I playfully shoved at his muscled chest, and he captured my wrist and tugged me closer, almost atop his lap. "Not the point." My lips twisted at the edges. "How long until you left?"

"You know . . ."

"You watched a few fights, didn't you?"

He squinted one eye, and I was sure he could feel the climb of my pulse in my wrist as he continued to hold me. "Maybe one or two."

"And where'd you go next that had you fleeing to come here?"

"Ethan chose the next place. Give you two guesses, but you'll only need one."

I thought about party-boy-Ethan. He'd finished grad school at Trinity not too long ago, and yet, he still hadn't slowed down. "Naked women, I'm guessing. A strip club."

"The only naked woman I want to see is you, so I didn't even go in."

"It's a bachelor party. Isn't it a requirement to have someone strip for you?"

He released my wrist and brought his thumb to my lip, gently pulling it down. He leaned closer, his mouth near mine. And everything inside of me became jelly. "Then you strip for me."

"Breaks the rules, doesn't it?" I lightly bit his thumb.

When my hand slipped to his lap, he was hard as a rock. The poor guy. What was I doing to him? To me?

Waiting until the wedding night would be worth it, I tried to remind myself, fighting the hot pulse of heat slowly crawling down my body like I was being unzipped. Ready to come undone.

I edged back enough to find his eyes. “Let’s leave.”

“Really?” His throat moved with a hard swallow.

I nodded. “If you think we can escape . . . I’m game.”

CHAPTER FOUR

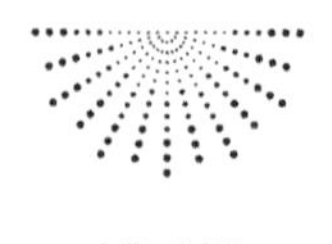

ADAM

"You're full of surprises."

I locked the hotel door and faced her, hands in my trouser pockets to fight the urge to pin her to the wall and ravage her.

She slipped off her heels and ate up the space between us. "How come we didn't have to check in downstairs?" One green eye narrowed. "Ohh. You already booked this room."

I observed her, trying to fight the smile that threatened as she figured it out.

"You knew I was at that club, didn't you?" Her hands went to her hips as if she could intimidate. Her pouty lips pressed together as she tried to get a read on me.

My cock throbbed in my pants as I held back.

We were inside the hotel—the exact room, to be precise—where we first made love.

"I've had it checked out for days now," I finally spoke.

"Anticipating I'd cave at some point?"

I shrugged, trying to maintain a sense of casualness, even though I was itching to lose myself in her. To take her into my arms.

She rolled her tongue over her teeth and wet her lips as

she stood before me. "I love you." Her fingers buzzed a path from my belt buckle up to the collar of my dress shirt. "Be with me."

A tightness stretched across my chest, a storm of emotions I'd never grow tired of experiencing because of her. She brought me back to life. Pulled me out of the darkness and into the light.

She bunched the hem of her bridal tee and pulled it over her head, tossing it behind her, revealing a white lace bra.

One step back. Eyes on me. She unclipped her bra.

"My own personal striptease?" My back was still to the door, and so I rested my head against it, watching my soon-to-be wife unzip her jeans and wiggle her hips as she shoved them down.

A tiny strip of white fabric was all she had on when her teeth skirted her bottom lip.

I finally lifted my hands from my pockets, no longer able to make this a spectator sport, and the memory of our first time together burned a hot trail through my mind.

I lowered my hand to her center and maneuvered her knickers to the side to touch her wetness. "Christ, woman."

I stole a moan from her lips with my mouth, and she pressed her tight body against mine and swept her hand between us. She covered my hand with hers, urging me to rub harder and faster, and I obliged.

I'd give her anything and everything to make her happy.

Our lips broke when her head rolled back as she came. I sucked at the sensitive part of her neck near her earlobe, loving every minute of how her body writhed in my arms.

"Oh damn, I needed that." She sighed and stepped back. "I didn't get off in the shower earlier like I was supposed to. Didn't have time."

Well, I had.

Twice.

Envisioning this moment to be exact.

She placed her hands on her hips. "What do you want to do with me now?"

My nostrils flared a touch as I studied her beautiful body. "So much," I said under my breath. "So. Damn. Much."

She squealed when I reached for her and tossed her over my shoulder, slapping her arse as I carried her to the connecting room.

I dropped her onto the bed, and her reddish-blonde hair fanned out beneath her head.

Her hands raced over my shirt, and she worked at the buttons as I held myself above her. I'd forgotten the inconvenience of my clothes, too wrapped up in the moment.

I hitched her thigh up and pinned her leg to my side, taking deep breaths as her eyes held mine. Owning me. All of me.

Once my shirt was open, her fingertips moved down my abs and to my buckle. "Why are you still dressed?"

"Feck if I know," I said with a laugh and stood to strip down to nothing.

Her lip caught between her teeth as she eyed me, her hand slipping to her breast, her tits puckering beneath my stare, and I grew even greedier with the need to have her. All of her.

"Best bachelor party ever." I grinned and lowered my now-naked body atop hers and hooked her leg up again as my cock settled at her opening. "You ready for me?"

"Always."

* * *

We took a left on to Grafton Street, and I parked my motorcycle.

She shook her mass of hair loose from the helmet and inhaled a breath of the fresh morning air.

"Breakfast in bed would've been fine, but—"

"We wouldn't have been eating," I said with a smile. "And you want to try waiting until the wedding again?"

"Yes. For real this time."

"Then I can't go near any beds with you." I reached into my pocket at the feel of my vibrating mobile and checked the ID.

"Who is it now?" Her smile stretched with amusement.

We'd both been getting hollered at via message since we'd bailed on the parties last night.

"Holly this time." I stowed the mobile and grabbed the helmets to carry.

"At least she gave up on me." She reached out, looped her arm with mine, and rested her head against my shoulder as we walked the footpath. "She was super distracted last night. Is she okay?"

"Distracted by what?"

"Work." She lifted her head, and I glimpsed her over my shoulder.

"That's nothing new, love. I wouldn't worry."

"If you say . . ." She stopped walking, and so I turned to see what was wrong.

"What's up?" I followed her eyes to St. Stephen's Green Park across the street.

She blinked and pulled her focus back to me. "Thought I saw someone I knew."

I reached for her elbow with my free hand and encouraged her closer to the side of a storefront out of the way of pedestrians. "What is it you aren't telling me? You look off."

"It's nothing. Some guy hit on me last night, and he reminded me of Jax."

Her ex. The son of a bitch I almost killed in Kentucky.

Heat torched a line up my spine, and my jaw clenched. "Why didn't you tell me last night?"

"I didn't want you to hit the guy."

"Did you spot him now?" I released her and looked toward the park again, my free hand converting to a fist at my side. My natural inclination always seemed to be to hit.

"I don't think so. It was dark at the club, and I'd been drinking. I'm sure whoever I saw in the park isn't him." She reached for my face and redirected my focus. "It's nerves," she said in a soft tone, trying to reassure me. "And now that we broke the no-sex-until-marriage rule, I'm probably nervous I jinxed us."

I shook my head. "Nothing is going to stop me from marrying you. That's a bloody promise." I couldn't help but check the park once more.

"The guy's gone. Whoever he was."

She sounded okay, so maybe I was overreacting. I relaxed my fingers, and she reached for my hand.

"Now, how about that breakfast?" she asked with a smile.

CHAPTER FIVE

HOLLY

"It's too late. They've already left." Sean reached for his wine glass and brought it to his lips, his eyes on mine. Regret appeared in the flecks of his irises as he studied me. "The meeting time was changed, and Da thought it'd be best for you not to come." The movement in his throat, the hard swallow, was a damn good indicator my brother was lying to me.

"Why?" My fingernails bit into my sides as I stared at him.

"Da's request." He shrugged, an attempt at casual. Too late.

I blew a few strands of hair out of my face as I stared at him. Feeling flustered. Not the norm for me. "Of all the times for Brian Callaghan to show up."

"Relax." He patted the air. "Da didn't sell."

"But he's thinking about it, isn't he?" I'd been doing my best to prevent the prick from getting face time with Da. "And why aren't you more bothered by this?"

"I am, which is why I made sure I was here."

I glanced down at the plates. A half-eaten steak on one.

Dried red blood stained the white china, the pink center exposed. Probably Da's food. He wasn't supposed to be eating red meat, but whenever Ma was out of sight, he did whatever he pleased regardless of his heart attack—a heart attack that happened a few weeks before Adam and Anna's original wedding date three months ago.

I rolled my eyes and turned to leave. I didn't want to talk to Adam about business so close to his wedding, but I needed to let him know what the hell was going on.

"Holly." Sean's voice was rough, like he'd choked on sandpaper. "I gotta pay the bill and hit the jacks. Wait for me."

"I need some air." I hurried toward the exit without waiting for his response and barreled into something just outside.

I glanced up at the man who had one hand on my shoulder, helping keep my balance, while he held a cigar in the other hand.

"Sorry." I edged back and out of his grasp. My bottom lip fell open as I averted my gaze up, and our eyes met. "Sebastian Renaud." I thought about the restaurant—*Les Fleurs*—it was his.

Did the man own everything in Dublin? He'd moved in like a storm from out of nowhere.

"I shouldn't have been standing right here. My apologies." His husky voice moved through the air and warmed me in all the right places, but I didn't want it to.

I took an extra step back to afford some space between us, but now I had the chance to observe his tall, muscular frame. Maybe not the best idea.

He raised the cigar to his lips, continuing to casually observe me.

“You know those things can kill you?” I folded my arms, not sure why the bleeding hell I was still standing there.

A slight smile tugged at the edges of his mouth as a dark brow rose. The lights from overhead the entrance cast him in some sort of glow, partially shadowing his face when he moved a little.

A fallen angel.

The devil.

A deal maker.

That was Sebastian Renaud. Well, from what I’d heard.

“Those heels of yours can be quite hazardous as well.” A hint of Dublin drifted through his speech despite the heavy sway of French wrapping around most of his syllables.

I looked down at my Michael Kors classic black heels. “They also double as a weapon when I’m walking the footpath alone.” I needed to turn away now, but then an idea, more like a desire, snapped right through me, and so I peered back at him. “You happen to have any cigs on ya?”

What am I doing? Shit.

He lifted his strong chin, and a ray of light returned over the part of his face that’d been hidden. “No, I don’t really smoke aside from an occasional one of these . . . but are ya sure you want to do something so dangerous?”

That slight smile did something funny to my ovaries.

But . . . wrong man. Wrong time. Wrong everything.

“I promised my older brother I wouldn’t smoke anymore, anyway. It’s been four years, but—”

“Adam or Sean? Who’d you promise?”

“You know who I am?”

“How could I not?” The memory of his eyes on me from the club during Anna’s bachelorette party swept back to mind.

“I should go,” I said, a bit too meekly for my liking.

At the sound of tires rubbing against the pavement, parking too close to the footpath, I turned to see a black limo. Probably his ride.

When I faced him again, he was in the midst of killing his cigar. "Goodnight, Miss McGregor." He brushed past me as he strode to the limo.

I waited for him to be out of sight before I dug into my purse for my mobile, hoping to shake off the strange feeling the man had given me: a feeling of . . . desire. Very misplaced desire.

I dialed my brother. "Adam?" I said straightaway when he answered, needing to get out of there before Sean came outside. "Where are you? We need to talk."

* * *

I SWUNG OPEN THE DOOR TO MY BROTHER'S GYM, AND I swear the place all but came to a complete standstill when I'd stepped inside.

I rarely came to his martial arts studio where he trained and worked with younger fighters. Adam's goal was to keep them off the streets and out of the reach of arseholes, like the one who had once tried to own Adam's soul.

I helped Anna design this place as a surprise for Adam, but my distaste for pounding flesh remained.

But right now, there was nothing more I wanted to do than curl my hand into a fist and knock it into one of those big black bag things, whatever they were called. To pretend it was Brian Callaghan's face in front of me so I could knock the bloke out.

Adam removed his gloves—the puffy ones, which meant he was boxing not doing that MMA stuff he normally did—

and he tossed them on a chair near the cage. "Hey, what's up?"

"Why are you even here a few days before your wedding?" I asked as he crossed his arms over his shirtless and sweaty chest. "You don't want to mess up your face."

He laughed a little. "I need to relieve some tension."

I didn't want to ask why, because well . . . brother.

"What has you so out of sorts?" He cocked his head.

"Da just met with Brian Callaghan. He's from Cork. Owns Callaghan Media Group."

Adam's eyes narrowed as if he were trying to locate some spark to help jog his memory.

"Callaghan's trying to make a play for MAC. It doesn't even make sense why Da would entertain meeting him, especially with such a lowball offer. But Callaghan won't quit. He's been coming at us pretty hard this last week. We were keeping you out of this nonsense because of the wedding, but I'm worried—"

"Wait. What?" He closed the gap between us and placed his hand on my shoulder, looking down at me with his brotherly blues. "You shouldn't have kept this from me. I'll call Da. I'll get this straightened out."

"No." The word came out more like an exhausted sigh at the realization of my mistake. "Damnit. I shouldn't have come here. I wasn't thinking straight. I'm sorry. You don't need this stress with the wedding."

"I'm going out of my mind waiting until the weekend." He opened his palms and glanced around the gym. "I could use something else to focus on."

"Are you sure? Selling our media division is an awful idea, but Da hasn't made the best choices since his heart attack, and so I'm worried he'll cave to Callaghan."

"We just took the company public a few months ago. I

can't imagine he'd make a move like this." He gently squeezed my bicep. "Let me handle it. Try and relax." His eyes journeyed over my shoulder, and I pivoted to see who had captured his attention.

"Hey," Anna said on approach. "What are you doing here?" She wrapped her arms around me for a quick embrace before shifting her focus to Adam. She kissed him despite the slight bit of sweat on his face.

"Business stuff." I forced a smile. "Nothing to worry about."

Adam held Anna against his side and continued to study me, a flicker of worry in his blue eyes. My family was going to be so pissed at me for involving him.

"You ready for the weekend?" At the feel of a vibration from a text, I searched my purse for my mobile.

"You know I'd be happy with something quick and easy, but this guy wants to give me the world, apparently." She looked up at Adam. "When are you going to realize you are my world?"

My stomach flipped a little at her words. I wasn't the most touchy-feely person. The only thing sugary I could digest were donuts once a month.

I barely heard Adam's response, too focused on the text that had just come through on my mobile.

Callaghan: *Your father didn't sign. Not yet, at least. Relax.*

Why did so many men keep telling me to relax?

Holly: *Get out of Dublin. Not a request.*

Callaghan: *Not going to happen.*

"You okay?" Adam asked as I shoved the mobile back into my purse. "You have that constipated look going on right now."

“Funny.” I rolled my eyes. “Just a message from the devil.”

Two devils in one night: Callaghan and Renaud.

“See you at the dress rehearsal Friday night.” I kissed Anna on the cheek goodbye, because I knew where I needed to go now, and it’s where I should’ve gone in the first place. “And, Adam?”

“Yeah?”

“Let me handle the Callaghan situation.”

CHAPTER SIX

HOLLY

"Do you live in this hotel, or do you own the place, too?"

"We keep running into each other. My club last weekend. The restaurant. Now here." Sebastian Renaud stood, adjusting his cuff links in the process. He turned his back to the bar in the lobby area of the hotel and fully faced me.

"That's not an answer." I crossed my arms, not sure why I was bothering to talk to this man for the second time in one night. I needed to find out which room Callaghan was staying in, but the women at the front desk couldn't be bribed.

Maybe seeing Renaud was fate. I didn't believe in that sort of thing, but . . . hell, I'd do what I had to do to make sure Callaghan stayed out of my life and out of the family business.

"Both." He tucked his hands into his trouser pockets. "I live here, and I own the hotel."

"Of course, you do." I resisted an eye roll since I was about to ask a favor. "Well, in that case, I need your help."

"With what?" His gaze wandered south of my face and to my blouse.

And why in the world did everything seem to come alive inside of me, like little neurons of energy firing up, whenever his eyes were on me?

I pressed a hand to my stomach, trying to gather my thoughts. To regain my focus. "I need to talk to one of your guests. Brian Callaghan. Can you tell me what room he's in?"

He lifted his hands from his pockets and pressed one palm to the bar counter at his side. His hands were rough. Masculine. Not the hands of a businessman who'd spent his days behind a computer.

"I can't give up information on my guests. My apologies, Miss McGregor."

I stepped closer to him. Dangerously close, maybe. Tempted to clutch the silk of his tie and tug.

His beard, probably a few days past due from being shaved, had me itching to touch it.

What's wrong with me? "I, uh, really need to talk to him. Give me his room number and—"

"And what, Holly?"

The way he said my name had my nipples straining against the fabric of my thin bra, and when his eyes dipped south again, I knew my blouse now showcased my arousal.

"Tell me, who made you quit?"

"What?"

His lips curved slightly at the edges when his eyes caught mine again. "Adam or Sean?"

Oh. The smoking. "Is this some form of manipulation tactic? What's your deal? If I answer will you give me the room number?"

Now his lips parted into a full-on smile. "Which question would you like me to answer first?"

I suppressed yet another eye roll, and tipped my chin so our eyes once again locked. I felt trapped and possessed by his brown eyes. "I should go." I tried to turn, but his hand wrapped around my wrist, and I stilled at the warmth of his touch. Scorching hot, more like it. "Sean," I sputtered, feeling the need to confess. "Adam never knew."

He kept hold of my arm, and I could feel the eyes of onlookers from the hotel as they observed us, or more likely him. A magnet who could probably draw everyone in. He was having that effect on me right now.

"You want to let go of me?"

"Not really," he replied. "But I'll help you."

"Yeah, and for what price?" I shirked free of the loose circle of his grasp.

"Let's just say you'll owe me a favor someday."

I moved back a step, nearly stumbling in my heels. "I don't like the sound of that."

"Relax." He tilted his head.

"I really am sick of that word." I shook my head. "But I'll take the room number, please."

"How about I escort you? That man isn't exactly someone you should be alone with."

I scoffed. "You're kidding, right? Have you looked in the mirror lately?"

A lazy grin met his lips as if amused by my comment. "I walk you or no deal."

"Fine," I grumbled, and he waved his hand in the air, motioning me toward the lift. "Do you need to look it up?" I asked as we made our way through the lobby.

"There are two presidential suites. I stay in one, and when I'm in town, I always know who's staying in the other." His voice was firm, and when I glanced at him out of the corner of my eye, I could see the hard strain of his jaw. "I assume this is a business visit, or you'd already know his room number."

"More like I'm trying to avoid business with the bast—" I cut myself off, realizing the man I was about to be alone with on my ascent was probably also a prick. I cleared my throat in a not-too-subtle way and stepped inside the lift once the guests cleared out.

My tongue traced a line over my bottom lip when our eyes connected in the mirrored doors on our way to the top level.

He fingered the collar of his crisp black dress shirt as if suffocating, but he kept hold of my eyes until the moment the doors parted.

"Which one is yours?" My gaze slid to the right to glimpse him.

He tipped his chin to the left. "Would you rather come to my place instead?"

I shrugged off the inconvenience of my yet-again misplaced desire and started for the right. "Not at all." But heading to Callaghan's room wasn't my idea of a good time, either.

Once at Callaghan's door, I rapped at it a few times.

Another three for good measure when there still wasn't an answer.

"Looks like he's not in," he said with a dash of arrogance, like he knew this was going to happen.

"Why'd you waste my time?"

"Have a drink with me. Tell me what you want from Callaghan, and I'll make it happen."

"Who are you?" I asked, unable to hide my curiosity. "For real."

He didn't answer. And he didn't need to. Because for some bloody reason I found myself trailing behind him toward his room.

I braced a hand on the frame of the open door a moment later, willing myself to walk away.

Don't go in there. How could I enter the fortress of the devil?

"This isn't a good idea." My voice was way too breathy, like I'd run a half marathon. Of course, I wasn't a runner, so what would I know? I was more of a yoga girl.

"What isn't a good idea?" He stood in front of his bar, holding a bottle of wine, and he pivoted to face me.

I strode over the line separating his room from the hall. No turning back now.

"Me being here." I huffed and closed the door behind me.

"Then why are you?"

I gulped back my discomfort and moved with unsteady legs farther into his room. "I need something stronger," I found myself murmuring, and a dangerously sexy grin touched his face.

This wasn't like me.

I wasn't weak or timid.

I didn't let a man control my thoughts or actions.

Worry over the Callaghan deal must've knocked me off my game, I surmised, hoping I was right. *Please be right.*

He crossed the short space between us and extended a drink. Bourbon. Well, that was stronger. Not my go-to, but I'd drink about anything at the moment.

The liquid burned my throat going down and warmed my chest.

He lifted a dark eyebrow and brought the rim of his drink to his mouth. "You better now?" he asked before swallowing the amber liquid.

I lowered my glass. "I will be when you tell me how you can help me."

He gestured with his glass toward the living area.

"I have a similar view," I said for some stupid reason when I settled onto a chair, my eyes on the windows. The dark sky like a warm blanket over the city.

"I figured, given who you are."

I considered his words when he sat across from me and leaned back in the chair. He rested his glass atop his thigh with his hand covering it. His dark eyes studied me. As if absorbing every fiber of my being.

It was unsettling. Mostly because I liked it.

I liked how I felt beneath the stare of his heavy-lidded eyes. His lust-filled eyes.

"So."

"So." His face remained stoic. "What's Callaghan done that's got you so upset?"

I didn't want to divulge business with a stranger, but for some reason I believed he could help me.

I'd owe him a favor, though.

I finished my drink and set it on the end table next to me. My hands slipped beneath my long hair and cradled my neck.

"Callaghan owes me a favor. I can call that favor in if you'd like. Just tell me what you need."

My arms fell at his words, and I braced my thighs. "Why do you want to help me? Don't give me this favor nonsense."

His head tilted. A flash of concern crossed his face, but I wasn't sure why.

I heaved out a deep breath and regained my focus. And my control. I straightened in my seat. "I need Callaghan gone. Off my back."

"What for?"

Damn him and his questions. Couldn't he help without details?

Adam and Anna were getting married Saturday. I didn't want anyone, especially Callaghan and my misguided father, ruining their day.

"He's coming after MAC," I said. "McGregor Advanced Communications," I clarified in case he didn't know the acronym for our media division. "I think he's using my father's recent heart attack to his advantage. A way to try and convince my father to sell to reduce stress."

He stood and approached the window. "And do you enjoy what you do?"

A crease in his shirt gathered at the center when his back muscles pinched together.

"Of course, I do." I stood and approached the window.

His free palm went to the glass, and he finished his drink before lowering it to his side. "I don't know if I believe you." When he faced me, his eyes were so dark, his pupils had nearly eclipsed all the color. "But I'll help you. I'll make Callaghan go away."

"I'm worried this favor I'll owe you will be much more significant than telling me his room number."

My BS meter wasn't going off, but I couldn't figure out a reason why a stranger—someone who knew more about me than I knew about him—wanted to help.

I took slow and deliberate breaths when he remained quietly observing me. "This was a mistake. I've changed my mind." I turned, but at the feel of his hand on my shoulder I chanced a look back at him.

"You sure about that?"

I forced a nod. "Yeah," I whispered. "Goodnight." I pulled free of his grasp and left his suite before I had a chance to change my mind.

I attempted Callaghan's suite one more time.

Impatience jetted through me as I waited for an answer.

My phone buzzed a moment later. A text.

My stomach lurched at the sight.

Sean: *Sorry . . . I couldn't stop him. Da just met up with Callaghan. They made a deal.*

CHAPTER SEVEN

ADAM

I'D DONE MY BEST TO HOLD MYSELF TOGETHER THROUGHOUT the parade of speeches delivered during the dress rehearsal dinner. I wasn't great at expressing myself publicly. Only when I was alone with Anna did I tend to find a level of comfort with such feelings.

"I can't believe tomorrow we'll be saying our vows beneath the sun on a hotel rooftop." Anna hooked her arms around my neck and lifted her chin.

She'd chosen the location because it had a stunning view of Trinity College—and she'd said she'd never forget the night we'd wandered the library there, and I'd made her feel like Belle from *Beauty and the Beast.*

Plus, River Liffey was not too far from the hotel—and *I'd* never forget the first time we'd laced hands and crossed the Ha'penny Bridge. I'd known at that moment, and probably even before, she was the one.

"Nothing bad happened," she whispered.

My brows drew inward. "Of course, nothing bad happened."

I couldn't mention the fight I had with Da today about

selling MAC. Nor could I tell her I'd been too afraid to truly lay into him at risk of causing a heart attack.

But how could Da agree to sell our media empire? And for such a shitty price?

McGregor Advanced Communications had been how I met Anna. She'd come from Kentucky for an internship, and neither of us had expected we'd end up marrying.

To hell with the company, though, I decided. Money didn't matter.

I was marrying Anna tomorrow.

If it weren't for how upset Holly was about the deal, I'd shirk the grip of guilt still clinging to me when I smiled at my soon-to-be -wife.

"Wait until you see the lingerie I have picked out for tomorrow night." She wet her strawberry-flavored, glossy lips with her tongue.

And like that, my thoughts and worries vanished.

Invitations. Cake samples. Photography. Flowers. All of the wedding details were a blur in my mind.

All I could think about was the moment Anna would walk down the aisle.

"In less than twenty-four hours you'll be my wife." I pressed my lips to hers.

"You got a great woman."

I begrudgingly pulled away from Anna to match a face to the voice. "Callaghan?"

The man adjusted the knot of his black tie and lifted a light-blond brow.

Anna turned to look at him. "Hi. You a friend of Adam's?" She extended her palm, and the cocksucker pressed his lips to her hand.

I circled her, knocked his arm away, and stood between them like a barrier. "Back off, Callaghan."

"What's going on?" she asked from behind.

"It's okay, sweetheart," Callaghan said. "Old Man McGregor invited me. To the wedding tomorrow, too. Surely you can make some last-minute arrangements to fit me in." His hands fell to his sides, and he stared at me with far too much confidence in the set of his light eyes.

Did the prick not know who the feck he was messing with? "Get out of here. Don't show your face tomorrow, either. It won't end well." I fought the urge to grab hold of his tie. To wrap my hands around his throat for making my sister miserable. For somehow taking advantage of Da.

Had my father lost his mind to invite the bloke to my wedding?

At the feel of Anna's hand on my back, I shifted my attention over my shoulder to observe her.

Concern flashed across her face. Exactly what I didn't want on the eve of our wedding. "Can you give me a minute?"

"Uh, sure." She left my side, retreating slowly toward the guests surrounding the open bar we had set up post-dinner.

"How'd you manage to snag a woman like her?"

The guy just wouldn't let up.

I grabbed hold of his shirt and bit down on my back teeth. "Get out of here. Now."

"Hey, what's going on?" Sean was on my left now, and I glanced at him without losing my grip. "Why the hell are you here? Haven't you done enough?"

"I was just asking him to leave," I seethed and returned my focus to the arsehole in front of me.

"I'm staying." He winked.

The fucker actually winked at me.

"Ask your father. See what he says." Callaghan peered at

something behind me, so I turned to follow his gaze. Da was there and talking to my buddy Marco.

When Da's eyes strayed from Marco to us, he almost immediately looked away.

"What do you have on him?" I finally let go.

He smoothed his hands down his shirt before stroking his reddish-blond beard. The son of a bitch was probably only a few years older than me. "Your father's getting old. I guess he'd prefer to sell off his company than leave one of you gobshites in charge."

"I advise you to shut your bleeding cakehole," Sean rushed out, and I observed him out of my peripheral view, noticing the hard clench of his jaw beneath his day-old stubble.

My twin was always clean-cut. Never a hair out of place. But since the Callaghan situation had turned our family business upside down, he'd been out of sorts.

"I'm not leaving." Callaghan reached for a flute of champagne off a tray when a server walked by us. "You better get used to me. I'm not going anywhere."

"Like hell you aren't. Not if I have anything to do with it," I said as I caught Anna's eyes from across the room and a band of discomfort stretched across my chest.

I couldn't let this man ruin our night or add any pre-wedding stress to my bride-to-be.

So, as much as it pained me, I walked away.

Holly blocked my path to Anna, and she rubbed her forehead. "I should've ended this the other night."

"What are you talking about?" I reached for her shoulder.

"I had a chance to force Callaghan to back off, but I was too afraid to make the move."

I needed to know more—to hear more, but when I saw Anna striding our way my heart worked into my throat. "I can't do this tonight," I said to my sister, hoping she'd understand.

"Of course." She followed my gaze. "The timing is horrible. I'm sorry." She patted my shoulder and averted her eyes to Anna.

I reached for Anna's hand and laced her fingers with mine, trying to lower my heart rate from nuclear to normal. "Sorry about that. There's nothing for you to worry about, though."

"Just business stuff," Holly came in for the save. "It's fine."

"You were grabbing his shirt." Anna bowed her head as if in silent prayer. "You were ready to pulverize him."

Truth or . . .? I looked to my sister, trying to find the words to make this night okay. To fix everything.

"Our father may sell MAC," Holly sputtered which had Anna's gaze snapping back up. "We're not in favor of the deal, and having that man here tonight of all nights—"

"Is he who you were texting the night of the bachelorette party? The reason why you were upset?" A form of clarity dropped over Anna's face, and Holly nodded.

"But we don't need to worry about the company this weekend." She reached out and squeezed Anna's hand. "Promise me you won't stress?"

I was almost surprised by my sister's gesture. I owed her one if this alleviated any of Anna's nerves.

"I'm not a bridezilla," Anna said with a smile. "You don't need to handle me with kid gloves." She turned toward me and lifted her palms to my cheeks. "I love you. You do what you have to do."

"And what I have to do . . . need to do . . . is marry you. And that's all I care to think about." I let go of a heavy breath.

"That's my cue to leave," Holly said.

My lips hovered before Anna's, and all my problems slipped away as I focused on her emerald-green eyes. "Marry me?"

"That's my plan." Her nose wrinkled and my lips closed in on hers, and I kissed her, my tongue flicking with hers.

Tomorrow she was going to be my wife and nothing in the world could stop that from happening.

CHAPTER EIGHT

ADAM

PRESENT DAY

"ANYTHING SUSPICIOUS YOU REMEMBER FROM THE LAST FEW days or weeks?"

My fingertips buried into my palms as I focused on the eyes of the detective. A memory catching in my mind. "A guy hit on her the night of her bachelorette party," I said slowly, guilt crossing through me. "And the morning after when we were walking, she said she thought she saw him again."

Could I have stopped this? Saved her?

"What club?"

I cleared my throat. "I—"

"I didn't see the guy at the club," Holly said, and I glanced over my shoulder to look at my sister in the hotel room. "But the club owner did. He, uh, rescued Anna from the jerk at the bar."

"Feck." My fingers tore through my hair as I lowered my head, trying to get a handle on everything.

Hours had already passed since I knocked on Anna's door. She could be anywhere. She could be . . .

No, I couldn't think of any alternative other than getting her back.

"We'll talk to the owner and pull the feeds from his club and see what we can come up with," Detective Grady said, his tone firm. "Where were you when she thought she saw the man again?"

"Grafton Street. Near the entrance to St. Stephen's Green. Around ten, maybe."

He took a note before his eyes traveled back to mine. A lot more than a flicker of concern as he studied me. Like he didn't think we'd be getting her back.

My stomach tucked in, grief carving out a hollow point.

"What about Brian Callaghan?" Holly came up alongside me.

"He got Da to agree to sell, so I can't imagine he'd have anything to do with this," I said.

"Yeah. Okay. He just creeped me out, so . . ." She rubbed her arms, goose bumps crisscrossing her skin.

"Callaghan?" There was something in the way the detective said the name that had my heart slowing.

"You know him?" I asked.

"We'll talk to him," is all he said, but there was more to it than that. I could bloody feel it.

"What is it? What aren't you telling me?"

"I'm sorry, I can't say more." Detective Grady looked at me. "If Callaghan has anything to do with this, though, we'll get to the bottom of it." His jaw briefly clenched. "You have my word. Everyone will be considered a suspect until we find her. Okay?"

"Callaghan's staying at a hotel nearby," Holly said, and I focused on her. "But he lives in Cork." Her lips pursed for a brief second. "He's staying at Sebastian Renaud's hotel, actually. Renaud owns the club we were at."

"I'm familiar with him." The detective's brows drew inward, and a darkness shadowed his eyes.

I resisted the impulse to grab him, to beat the information out of him.

He rolled his lips inward, his mustache going with it before he lifted his eyes to mine.

"Is this Renaud guy a suspect, too?" My heart raced. My pulse climbed. I was ready to tear out of the hotel to talk to Renaud myself.

"We'll look into him." He nodded. "Like I said, we'll look into everyone." His throat moved with a hard swallow, his Adam's apple rolling beneath the skin.

"They'll find her." Holly reached for my arm but nothing would steady my pulse.

"We checked Anna's room for prints. Same with her mobile." Detective Grady shook his head to let me know they came up empty. "I have my people going through her contacts, but if you can make a list of everyone she saw regularly—especially recently, that'd speed up the process."

"Of course." I lifted my mobile from my pocket, my hand trembling a touch. "Why hasn't anyone called yet? If this is for a ransom wouldn't they have called by now?"

"We have to give it time," he said. "But we know Anna got out of this room somehow. Our team's analyzing the security feeds now. Whoever messed with the cameras is a pro, that's for sure."

His words sure as hell didn't make me feel better.

The detective's eyes winged to Holly's face before connecting with mine again. Additional worry lines added to the wrinkles on his forehead. "If you don't get a call within twenty-four hours, this is probably not a ransom situation."

This wasn't a fecking situation. This was the love of my life.

"Get me that list." He nodded. "I have to make some calls. Be back in twenty for it." He left the room, and a few other officers trailed behind him.

"I'm so sorry," Holly said softly.

"I can't sit around and wait for them to figure out where she is." My hand converted to a fist. "I should go to the club. Talk to Renaud. Callaghan, too." The sound of my mobile ringing had me dropping my words, and my heart stammered.

I hung my head at the sight of the familiar number.

Not a ransom call.

"It's Marco. His friends must be here."

"Friends?" She cocked her head.

"Hey," I answered.

"We're in room twenty-one-ten. Can you come down?" Marco asked.

"On my way." I ended the call. "Marco has some people who might be able to help," was the only explanation I offered before rushing out of the room, assuming she'd follow.

"The detective won't like this," she said once we were alone in the lift.

"I'm sure the detective's good, but we need all the help we can get." My eyes met hers in the mirrored lift doors. "I can't . . . I can't lose her." My voice wavered as emotion cut through.

"We'll find her." She reached for my arm and squeezed. "I promise." She released her hold once the doors parted, and we headed to the hotel room.

Marco already had the door open, waiting for us at the end of the hall. He ushered us inside, and my stomach lurched at the sight of computers and weapons unpacked in the room.

This was all too real now.

A brunette was at the desk with two laptops in front of

her, and my heart skipped into my throat at what was on the screens. She'd managed to access the hotel security cameras already.

"This is Alexa Ryan," Marco said, and I assumed she'd once been the MI6 officer, given how deftly her fingers moved over the keys.

She peered at me from over her shoulder, her hazel eyes catching mine without breaking stride from her work. "I'm so sorry about what happened." Her lids fluttered closed briefly before she looked at me again. "We'll get her back."

"Thank you," I said as she refocused on the screen.

"Jake Summers." A guy approached with an extended hand, so I turned to greet him. "Alexa's my fiancée, and she's the damn best at pretty much everything." He was American. Southern by the sounds of it.

His dark-brown eyes thinned as I shook his hand. I contemplated a response, but the words remained lodged in my throat, so he shifted his attention to my sister.

"Holly McGregor."

"Sorry to meet you under these circumstances, ma'am," Jake said.

"I'm just glad you can help." Her gaze flitted to Marco standing tensely in the room by the door as if he didn't know what the hell to do.

That made two of us.

"That's Xander." Jake jerked a thumb toward a man crouched in front of a duffel bag.

"I worked with Alexa for Her Majesty," Xander said. "And now—well, we do this. Bring down bad guys. Help people." He was British like Alexa. And if Xander had been in a suit, he'd look like James Bond. And I needed a hero right about now. "We'll find her."

I nodded my thanks.

Xander's gray eyes swept over to Holly for a brief moment, and he gave her a quick smile.

"Maybe you can start from the beginning," Jake requested, and I focused back on him as he crossed his arms and observed me, a visible strain to his jaw.

The guy looked military. Probably once was. And I was glad I had these people in my corner. Well, in Anna's corner.

Marco motioned for me to sit, but I didn't budge. I felt immobile. A fixture of the hotel room.

I'd never felt so fecking horrible in all my life.

And I couldn't begin to imagine what was happening to Anna right now.

My lungs burned, and I fought to keep it together. I was on the verge of losing it as tears formed in my eyes.

Men weren't supposed to cry, were they?

But this was Anna.

Anna was everything to me.

"I know this is hard, but every detail you can provide will help us track her down," Jake said, and I suddenly realized I recognized this man from the news.

Jake had helped foil a massive terrorist attack back in 2017. He was a former FBI agent and once a special operations Marine.

I dragged my palms down my face, the texture not as rough since Anna had insisted I fight with gloves to keep my hands and knuckles in decent shape for the wedding.

"From the moment you met Anna to this morning—don't leave anything out." Xander was now on his feet alongside Jake.

I blew out my cheeks and released the breath. "Well, it all started when she came to Dublin to work at my company as an intern . . ."

CHAPTER NINE

ADAM

"He looped the feeds to cover his tracks," Alexa said shortly after I returned from meeting with the detective. "He had a ball cap on and hid his face from every camera in the hotel."

"That doesn't sound easy to do," Holly said, standing off to my left.

"It's not. In fact, he was so damn good at it, I almost missed it," Alexa said.

"Which means the man has off-the-charts tech and cyber skills," Jake noted. "That's an important detail when we're creating a person of interest list."

I couldn't get any words out—my eyes were glued to Alexa's screen when she displayed a man exiting the hotel room pulling a large rolling duffel bag behind him.

The red fabric had my chin dipping as I took measured breaths, trying to stay calm when all I wanted to do was throw my hand through a wall.

"Oh, God." I peered over at my sister after she'd spoken. "Anna's in that bag, isn't she?"

The idea of Anna's body being in the luggage . . . it was

as if the tips of knives slowly scraped up the center of my body and a final cut across my throat was imminent.

I felt like death was on the verge of eclipsing my life. Stealing the soul I now knew I had because of Anna.

"He brought her out of the hotel in that suitcase," I echoed my sister's line of thought before anyone had answered her.

When I focused my attention back on the computer, my stomach did a full-on freefall. A much worse gut-punch sensation than the time my main parachute had failed when I jumped from a plane.

"Looks that way," Jake said as fast as possible as if the taste of the words burned across his tongue.

"But was she alive when he put her in that bag?" I had to ask, but damned if I didn't want any answer other than *yes*.

I gripped my chest, wanting to squeeze my heart, to rip the organ from my body.

"We believe so," Xander said. "If he, uh, killed her first, I don't think he would've gone to such lengths to hide the fact he was there."

"Unless he wanted you to think she ran away for some reason," Xander said. "But I doubt it."

Xander's words produced a hard look from Jake. A warning shot. A near knock-out punch with only his eyes.

Jake wanted me to keep it together, and if I already thought she could be dead . . .

I turned from everyone in the room and scrubbed both palms down my face, trying to maintain a sense of calm. The calm before the storm.

"This guy had to be on-site when he did this. He couldn't have screwed with the footage like this from somewhere else. He had to be near the servers in the hotel to pull this off, which means he came back into the hotel after he took Anna out," Alexa said, and her words had me looking back at her. "It's possible he covered all of his tracks, but I'll comb through every feed to find any anomalies."

"I assume the cameras outside the hotel aren't of any use?" I asked after gathering my focus, willing the pain to take a back seat so I could find my fiancée. "Or the cameras at Renaud's nightclub?"

"I'm also working on traffic cams," she began. "But as for the club, the guy talking to Anna at the bar kept his back to the cameras. The lighting is shit, but he's got the same build as our guy exiting Anna's room."

"So, it could be him?" I asked as she switched camera angles to showcase the outside of the club.

Anna was standing in line with her bridal party, and my chest tightened at the sight of her.

"We don't know for sure," Jake said. "But we do know Brian Callaghan was outside the club the night of her bachelorette party."

I closed in on the screen and braced Alexa's chair as I eyed Callaghan standing on the other side of the street, leaning against a black limo. "Callaghan was there?" I breathed out, my words a ghostly whisper of disbelief.

I'd mentioned Callaghan's name, among others, when I'd given them the rundown.

"It can't be a coincidence," Alexa said.

"We're running the plate number of the limo," Jake said. "We'll make sure we talk to the driver."

Thank God for them. I'd never be able to sit back and let the Garda handle this and remain in the dark.

"I don't understand how Callaghan even knew we'd go there, and at that time, no less," Holly said. "I need to talk to Kate. It was her idea to go to that club." I looked over at her, and she rubbed at her forehead. "I was even texting Callaghan while we were in there. It's just all so strange."

"Does this mean he's moved up higher on the suspect list?" I still couldn't figure out why the hell Callaghan would take Anna, especially when he got Da to agree to sell.

Alexa looked at Jake, and it was as if there was a silent conversation happening between them. She cleared her throat and redirected her gaze my way. "Honestly, whoever took Anna went to great lengths to keep his identity protected."

"So Callaghan's face on camera doesn't jive," I finished her line of thought.

"But that doesn't mean he's not caught up in all of this somehow," Jake said.

"Or someone wants us to think that," Xander added, and my mind was beginning to spin again. "We should check your car, Holly, to see if someone put a tracker on it. Someone had to have known where you were going that night."

"We took a limo to the club," she replied.

"You meet with Callaghan any time before the party?" Alexa asked while working at the keys again.

"He could've mirrored your phone," Jake said.

"No, but uh . . . mirror?" She sat on the couch in front of the window which overlooked the river.

"He may have cloned your mobile," Xander explained.

She snatched her purse and retrieved her mobile and offered it to Jake. "We never met face-to-face until the dress rehearsal dinner last night. Sean and Da did, though, but they didn't know where we were going for the bachelorette party." She shook her head. "I'm sorry." Her apology was directed at me, as if she were somehow responsible for what happened.

"This isn't on you." *Probably me, though.*

"We'll take a look at your phone just in case." Jake

handed it off to Alexa. "We need to go talk to Callaghan and Renaud."

"I'm coming," I rushed out.

"The cops might be with him right now." Jake checked his watch. "It's the afternoon, so I doubt Renaud's at the club. We can head to his hotel and scope the place out. But let Xander and me go in first before you show your face. I don't want the police pissed at you for interfering with their investigation."

"They'll have to lock me up to stop me from looking for Anna."

"I should come, too," Holly said. "I've been to Renaud's home before."

My thoughts scattered at her words. A delayed blush appeared on her skin.

"I was seeking Callaghan, trying to reason with him about coming after the company, and I ran into Renaud at the hotel. He brought me to Callaghan's room, but he wasn't there, and so . . ."

I ate up the space between us, my heartbeat losing its normal rhythm. "What happened? He didn't fecking hurt you, did he?"

"No." Her brows knitted. "We talked. He offered to get rid of Callaghan for me."

"Get rid of him? In exchange for what?" Alexa swiveled in the chair to view her.

"A future favor. I don't know. He was vague." She lifted her shoulders. "And I said *no*, so . . ."

Jake looked to Xander. "Yeah, we better talk to this guy."

Xander holstered a sidearm and covered it with his shirt.

"Let's roll out." Jake motioned for the door. "Call us if you find anything," he said to Alexa.

Part of me wanted to tell him to drop what he was doing

and marry her. Don't delay. Don't waste one damn minute. Because you never know what might happen next.

But the greedy part of me needed their help, so I'd save my soapbox speech for when Anna was safe.

* * *

"The Garda haven't gone to Renaud's hotel, yet," Alexa said over speakerphone not even ten minutes after we'd parted. "Looks like you're going to beat them to it."

The tap-tap-tap of the keyboard in the background competed with the thumping of my heartbeat as I waited to hear more.

"Why haven't they gone there yet?" *What the hell are they doing, damnit?*

"Looks like they're trying to rule out the Donovan Hannigan revenge angle first," she replied.

The idea had crossed my mind since Detective Grady had brought it up earlier, but I wasn't sure who in Hannigan's old circle would have the balls or the means to do such a thing as to take Anna from me, not without a death wish. "And how do you know all of this?"

"She's a cyber queen," Xander said, sitting in the back seat of my Audi. "*The* cyber queen."

"We'll let the police focus on the Donovan Hannigan connection then," Jake said, which meant he must've assumed it was a dead lead.

Jake was driving my car, and thank God he'd offered. I'd probably have gotten us into an accident.

My brothers were still aimlessly roaming the city as if they'd somehow spot Anna walking down Grafton. God, I could only hope. But they were trying to help; they couldn't sit idle with her missing.

Anna's dad was out there, too. He didn't know his way around the city, but this was his daughter, and nothing would stop him from trying to find her.

"I did find a link between Brian Callaghan and Sebastian Renaud," Alexa announced.

"What?" I nearly snatched the mobile from where it was mounted on the dashboard as Jake parked.

"It was one of Renaud's drivers chauffeuring Callaghan the night of the party," Alexa said.

"You talk to the driver yet?" Jake asked.

"No answer. I'm working on it. But apparently, Callaghan always uses Renaud's hotels, and his other places of business whenever he's in town."

Jake killed the engine. "Did you get Renaud and Callaghan on camera together?"

"Yeah, talking at his hotel bar, but that could be a coincidence since it's Renaud's place."

"Who the hell is this guy?" Holly asked.

"I don't know because Renaud didn't exist until five years ago," Alexa answered. "Whoever Renaud was before—he did a hell of a job at burying that person."

"If he's capable of that, is he also capable of looping the camera feeds at the hotel?" I asked, wondering if this son of a bitch was somehow behind Anna's abduction.

"He looks nothing like the man we saw on camera outside Anna's hotel room," Holly said. "Renaud is taller. More muscles."

"He probably would've hired someone to do his dirty work." I expelled a hard breath. "I assume whoever hit on Anna at the bar, too, could be a—"

"A plant," Alexa interrupted. "Someone to divert our attention."

"Or the guy from the bar is unrelated. Just some creep

hitting on her," Xander said. "We have to look at every angle with an open mind."

Jake nodded. "Renaud, Callaghan—they may not have Anna. But they're connected to everything somehow," he said in a low, bone-chilling voice.

I scratched at the stubble I never got a chance to shave this morning before the wedding.

Anna had been worried we'd jinx the day, and now . . .

My thoughts winged to the dark corners of my mind. To the place where I'd stuffed away the morbid ideas of what could be happening to her.

Each thought had me growing lightheaded. Dizzy. Ready to collapse and give in to the pain.

But no. Damnit. I was a fighter, wasn't I?

No matter how much I'd tried not to be.

And Anna would fight, too. She wouldn't let someone beat her down. She was strong. Resilient.

I rubbed at the growing achiness in my chest and shoved the door open. "We're getting her back today," I said as a command, needing for it to be true.

"The first twenty-four hours are the most critical," Jake said after ending the call with Alexa a moment later.

Xander tipped his chin in the direction of the hotel. "Then let's do this."

CHAPTER TEN

HOLLY

It wasn't my fault, and yet, I couldn't help but feel responsible.

I'd been in Renaud's home. I'd desired him. Wanted him to screw me six ways to Sunday, even though it'd felt wrong. Dirty.

"Kate just got back to me," I said after reading the text. "She said going to Renaud's club wasn't the original plan. She met some guy three nights prior to the bachelorette party, and he invited her to Renaud's place Friday night, and so, she switched the location of the party in hopes of seeing him there."

I handed Jake my mobile to show him the information Kate had provided. The description of the guy, the time, and place. "You think that guy's our kidnapper then?" I asked Jake as he forwarded the details to Alexa.

"Let's hope so, because we can pull surveillance from the bar Kate first met him at," he answered.

"Unless the bastard kept his face hidden there, too," Adam said, a grim tone to his voice.

"Let's try and be positive." Jake handed the mobile back to me.

"Renaud. Callaghan." I whispered their names under my breath as we ascended. "None of this makes sense. But so help me, if either of them hurts Anna I'll kill them myself."

Xander peeked at me from over his shoulder. His eyes the color of steel. "I'll hold him down while you do it if that's the case." I could feel the hard sting of his words. It didn't appear to be his first time dealing with death. "But let's get Anna back without anything happening to her."

Adam didn't say a word; how could he? His mind had to be racing in so many different directions, and surely all tracks led back to a perfect storm of grief and anger. And I knew my brother, he'd destroy anyone who even touched Anna.

"*Les Fleurs*," I whispered as a memory grabbed hold of me. "Sean and Da met up with Callaghan at that restaurant this past week. I bumped into Sebas . . . er, Renaud there that night. He also owns that place."

"Too many coincidences." Adam's tone converted to a half growl as he spoke.

When the doors parted, Xander asked, "Callaghan or Renaud first?"

"Renaud," Jake said, and a few seconds later, we knocked on his door.

My heart wedged into my throat, temporarily obstructing my airway when the door opened inward.

Worn-out jeans and a white tee—a look I hadn't anticipated on a man like him. His broad shoulders filled out the shirt, the same way his biceps fought with the fabric of the sleeves.

Renaud met my eyes. Looking at me as if I were the only one standing before him.

"I was expecting you." He stepped back, offering us

entrance, and a cold bristle of air flowed up my spine when I moved past him then turned around.

He scratched at the back of his neck and faced us once the door was closed.

Everything had me on edge just being within arm's reach of him. And so, I backed the hell up, nearly bumping into the hall table.

"Please, have a seat." He motioned toward the living area of his massive suite, a room fit for a king, and apparently, Renaud. "I'm sorry to hear about your fiancée, McGregor."

Adam didn't sit, and neither did Jake nor Xander.

We weren't there for a social call, but I wasn't sure if my legs would hold my weight beneath his heated stare. Even when I turned my back toward him, I could still feel his eyes on me. Like he'd stripped me naked and was currently memorizing every curve of my body.

"So, you know why we're here?"

At the sound of the rough texture of my brother's voice, I swiveled back around to face everyone, worried Adam might lose control.

He moved closer to the man, and Adam's tall height managed to fall slightly shy of Renaud's towering frame. "Do you know where she is? Did you have anything to do with this?" he seethed, his hands bunching at his sides.

"Adam." Jake stood behind him and placed a hand on his shoulder, urging him to back down. And Xander flanked Adam's side.

Three to one. Not a fair fight, even though I sensed Renaud could hold his own.

I stood awkwardly off to the side of the men, willing my thundering heart to calm the bloody hell down.

I wanted to sit, but I also refused to get comfortable, and so, I folded my arms and seized in a breath—with it, came Renaud's cologne, the dark notes flitted to my nostrils.

The hotel room smelled like him.

The place was dark and cold. And so, it felt like him, too.

My skin itched with the need to leave.

My body was a betrayal to Anna. She was missing, and yet, this man somehow had lit a fire inside of me this past week, and it seemed to rage and burn harder, hotter, and faster even now.

I hated him for it.

Hated myself even more.

It'd only been seconds since Jake had requested Adam to back away from Renaud, but the lapse of time had felt like a space of eternity to me.

I needed to get out of there and away from him.

"I'm not responsible. And Callaghan may be an arse, but I'm pretty sure he didn't take Anna." His Irish tongue took a front seat to his half-French background. Well, if the man really was part French. What if his entire history had been one big lie?

What if he wasn't even Irish and—

"How could you possibly know what Callaghan's capable of?" Adam asked, a harsh grit in his tone, interrupting my thoughts.

"Well, Callaghan's also now a dead arse." His gaze moved past the men as if they weren't standing before him like a wall. He'd managed to find a glimmer of space to catch my eyes—and apparently, I'd done the same.

And it took me a moment to process what he'd said. "Dead?" I whispered and averted my attention to the floor.

"What are you talking about?" Jake spoke this time.

"He wasn't answering my calls, and so, I used my key to check out his room. Found him dead. Stabbed three times."

The way he'd said the words it was as if he didn't have a caring bone in his body.

My stomach roiled. This was all way too much.

"Are the Garda on their way?" I asked, wondering how Alexa wouldn't have known that given her crazy cyber skills.

"Not yet, I was about to phone them when you knocked on my door."

I opened my mouth, but he lifted his hand and lightly shook his head. "And no, I don't think it's a good idea for you to go in there and see him."

I couldn't get my mouth to move, too focused on the dark gleam of Renaud's eyes.

A lone lamp was all we were working with since the wall of curtains sealed out any natural light, but it was all I needed to see him.

To see the darkness in his eyes.

The potential evil.

"You did it, didn't you?" I accused. "*You* killed him." I nearly choked on my question when his eyes swept over my body like the touch of expensive satin on my skin.

"No. Sorry to disappoint you." He faced Jake. "He owed me. So, no, I didn't want him dead. I can't collect on my debt now."

His words were the only thing casual about the moment. As if the man's death was an inconvenience and nothing more.

Who are you? "Owed you what?"

"The details of my relationship don't matter, Miss McGregor. Callaghan liked to stay at my hotel and use my drivers whenever he came to town. He always went to my places of business. He felt safe under my protection, since he wasn't the most loved man."

"Looks like it got him killed," Jake grumbled. "How long ago did you find the body? Five minutes? Ten?"

Renaud's chest rose and fell with a deep breath. "About an hour ago."

"What?" Adam moved closer to him.

Renaud adjusted the silver watch band on his wrist before his eyes swept north to find my face. "I wanted to check the cameras before I called the Garda. To see who went into the room."

"You tamper with evidence, too?" A hard beat of authority moved through Jake's tone.

"Of course not, but I can't have someone murdering guests in my hotel without—"

"Who'd you see on camera?" Adam interrupted. "Who went to his room before you?" His fingertips tucked into his palms at his sides. The pulse pricked at the side of his neck; he was ready to lash out at anyone right now.

"Your father," he answered after a moment.

"What?" Adam rubbed at his right temple and bowed his head.

Jake edged closer to Renaud, taking charge of the situation, and thank God for him. Adam and I could handle a lot of things—but Anna being kidnapped and now a murder . . . no way. "The police will know you went into the room an hour ago," he said. "Why take the risk and wait? You've now earned yourself a top spot on the suspect list. Hell, you may have bumped Adam's father's name with your own."

"Or maybe it was you who killed Callaghan," Xander suggested.

Renaud turned away from us. "They won't be focused on me, I can promise you that."

"And how can you be so certain?" Jake asked.

"Because Callaghan was blackmailing your father."

Renaud faced us again, a grim twist to his lips, as if he didn't want it to be true.

"How do you know?" Adam asked before I could.

"There was an envelope in Callaghan's room," he replied.

"What was in it?" I moved closer to Renaud and reached out for his arm.

His gaze dropped to my hand. "That's irrelevant. I don't believe your father killed him, but it sure as hell looks that way now. You should focus on finding Anna, then clear your father's name before it's too late."

I considered his words, my thoughts wandering to my conversation with Renaud earlier this week. "You knew why Callaghan was in town, didn't you? You knew about the blackmail before today. When we spoke that night—"

"He never told me."

I let go of his arm and closed my eyes. "What else aren't you telling us?" Desperation broke through my voice.

Adam couldn't lose her.

I couldn't lose her. I wanted her as a sister, and . . .

"Please," I begged. "We have to find her." Emotion rose to the surface, and even if I was uncomfortable with showing such a display, I couldn't hold it back. "If you know anything, help."

"I called the limo driver Callaghan had been using this past week after I found his body. I wanted to see what the hell Callaghan's been up to," he began. "He mentioned Callaghan asked him to park outside my club last Friday and wait. Then he said Callaghan got a call, he stepped out of the limo, met with some guy who handed him an envelope, then he came back to my hotel."

"The envelope," Adam said. "Is that how Callaghan got the blackmail?"

"I assume." Renaud rubbed his jaw. "His driver didn't see

a face. Just said the guy had short brown hair and was in jeans and a black tee."

"We've been trying to reach the driver," Jake said. "We should talk to him."

Renaud nodded. "He's downstairs in the lobby right now."

"What are the odds Callaghan happened to be at your club for the exchange at the same time Anna showed up for the bachelorette party?" Xander interjected, and all eyes went to him.

"Did you phone the prick to let him know Anna would be there?" Adam grated out. "Did you—"

"No, of course not," Renaud interrupted. "I noticed Holly that evening, but I had no clue the party was happening at my club before then."

"Someone wanted Callaghan there, though," Jake said. "And they waited for Anna to arrive to make sure we got Callaghan and Anna on camera at the same time."

"Sounds like whoever has Anna killed Callaghan and is looking to pin the blame on your father," Renaud said.

"I'm still wondering if you're involved." Adam's eyes thinned as he observed Renaud.

"I have nothing to gain from any of this," he said. "And although my security cameras are top of the line, I'm betting they've been tampered with to hide the real killer's entrance and exit into Callaghan's room."

"It'd fit the abductor's M.O.," Xander said. "If Renaud's telling the truth, then I think Anna's abduction isn't about you, Adam."

"What are you saying?" Red streaks advanced up Adam's neck and to the tips of his ears.

Xander's hands settled on his hips. "I think whoever has her—well, they might just be out to get your whole family."

CHAPTER ELEVEN

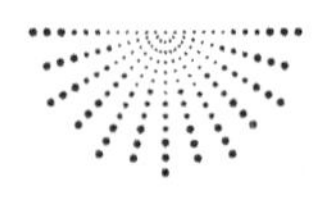

ADAM

I SLAMMED MY FIST AGAINST THE DOOR AT THE STATION AND whirled around to face Detective Grady.

Renaud, Holly, and I had been escorted from Renaud's hotel and asked a shit-ton of questions. Xander and Jake had slipped away to continue working before the Garda had arrived.

Da was there now, too. Locked inside one of the interrogation rooms next to where they were interviewing Renaud. Holly and I had been let go fairly quickly.

"Callaghan's killer has Anna. You're wasting time questioning my father!" I snapped.

"You should go," Grady said in a low voice. "Try and get some rest until we know more."

"Rest?" I faked a laugh. "Someone is now framing my father for murder. The same someone who probably has Anna." My hands went to my hips. "So, no, I don't think I'll be resting."

He held his palms in the air. "You've been through a lot. I know this is hard for you, but—"

"Hard for me?" Now I was really going to lose it. "Hard

for me was nearly paralyzing a fighter when I was younger. This is fucking hell. More than hell. This is the end of the world. Anna is gone. She could be . . ." My voice broke, cutting off my ability to finish my line of thought.

Anna had to be alive. I refused to accept any other outcome than her return.

"My fiancée is missing," I said when I regained my focus. "And now you think my father could be a killer." The words were absurd. "Someone wanted it to look like my family thought Callaghan took Anna because he was blackmailing us."

"So, you know about the blackmail?" His forehead tightened. "Your father tell you that or Renaud?"

"If Da was guilty, why would he leave the blackmail behind in Callaghan's room?"

He leaned back in his dress shoes and crossed his arms. "My theory's that your father got pissed about the blackmail, and then he went to the hotel and accused Callaghan of kidnapping Anna. They fought, and your father killed him."

"Well, your theory is total bullshit." I turned and dragged my palms down my face, catching sight of a man being escorted in by officers.

"Who is he?" I asked; he looked vaguely familiar.

"Renaud's limo driver. We have some questions to ask him."

Yeah, me, too. The driver hadn't been in the lobby like Renaud had said when the Garda had shown up for Callaghan's body. At least they found him, though.

I swallowed a lump in my throat, and then I faced the detective again. He toyed with the gold band on his wedding finger, and my eyes nearly bulged at the sight, at the reminder of what today was supposed to be.

Acid burned a hole in my stomach as I fought away

images of Anna being hurt. The ideas kept blanketing my mind all day, strangling the breath from my throat.

"What about the driver?" I asked. "What if he lied to Renaud about a guy handing off the envelope?"

Or Renaud lied about all of it? Shit, I didn't know what to think.

"It's possible the driver was the one who actually provided Callaghan with the blackmail," I pointed out. "Maybe the blackmail even came from Renaud. Feck." I raked my hands through my hair. "Any of them could be involved! Everyone could be lying."

"Adam, what's going on? How do you know all of this?"

I'd forgotten Grady had no idea I'd called in reinforcements. I shouldn't know what I did, and it'd have the detective only asking more questions. And what I needed was for him to focus on Anna.

Instead of answering him, I looked at the room where Da was being questioned.

When the door to that room opened a second later, I caught sight of Da. His head was bowed. Eyes closed.

My entire body tensed, and I staggered back a step as the detective shut the door behind him and found my eyes.

"We got a confession," the man said.

"He confessed?" Grady took a folder from the other detective and opened it.

No way could I have heard him right.

"Maybe next time you tell me in private instead of in front of the son of a suspect," Detective Grady hissed.

My body grew rigid, the fight inside of me building more intensely. "You need to find Anna." I fisted the detective's shirt and pulled him closer to me. "Da isn't a killer. This is a distraction. Don't you feckin' get it?"

Officers grabbed hold of my arms and pulled me back,

but I wouldn't let go. I'd mow down anyone who stood in my way to get to Anna.

"It's fine." The detective lifted his chin, ordering the officers to back off. "He's upset."

I released him after a moment and shook my arms loose at my sides once they removed their hands from me. "He didn't kill anyone, and you know that." I swallowed. "Did you check the security footage outside Callaghan's hotel room to see if it was tampered with?"

Grady rubbed at his jaw.

"What about my hotel?" I asked when he didn't answer. "The security footage showed a guy leaving Anna's room with a duffel bag."

He cocked his head. "I'd still like to know how in the bleeding hell you know so much?"

I turned and braced the back of a rolling chair at a nearby empty desk.

I had to get out of there. To get back to Jake and the others. I needed them now more than ever.

I couldn't trust these people to do their job, not with someone out there three steps ahead of us at every turn.

No. I had to find Anna. Right the hell now.

* * *

"WHERE'S XANDER AND JAKE?" I ASKED ONCE IN THE HOTEL room and took a second to catch my breath after charging up several flights of stairs. I had to take the back entrance to avoid the reporters still staked out at the front of the hotel. Word had spread fast Da had just been arrested for Callaghan's murder.

"We ID'd the guy who hit on Kate, the man who invited her to Renaud's club. Xander and Jake went to question him," Alexa explained. "Hopefully they'll be back soon."

Thank God for something. "What about my father?"

She turned in her chair to face me. "They uploaded his confession twenty minutes ago. According to the report, your father and Callaghan got into a fight, and your dad stabbed him multiple times with a pocket knife."

"A pocket knife?" I shook my head. "Da doesn't carry a damn pocket knife around with him."

"This is total bullshit." Holly rose from the bed where she'd been sitting. "Why would he confess to killing him, though?"

Alexa's face pinched tight. "Your father got a text from an anonymous number two hours ago. The message said if he didn't show up at Callaghan's hotel room, Anna would be killed. And if he told anyone," she began, "well, you get the idea."

"Jesus." That explained why Da had been MIA in the last few hours. "How could the Garda not realize this?"

"Because the text was deleted," Alexa said. "And unless the police thought to dig deep, they wouldn't have discovered it."

"So, someone wanted Da there, but do you think Callaghan was dead before Da got to the hotel?" Holly asked, her voice soft.

"The killer may have let him in. Planted the evidence. And then threatened to kill Anna—you guys, too, for all I know—if he didn't confess to the murder," she explained. "But I do know for certain Callaghan was a pawn in all of this."

"What do you mean?" I edged closer to her desk.

"I was able to pull up all of Callaghan's last calls, texts, and emails. Someone attempted to delete the records from cyber space, but I managed to recover them," she said. "Callaghan had been in contact with someone who promised him blackmail, which would help him acquire your media business for cheap."

"Can you track the number?" I asked.

"I'm working on it, but whoever we're dealing with is a professional. He knows how to cover his tracks." She gave a light nod. "But I'm better," she said with confidence. "So I'll find him."

I had to cling to the hope we were close to the truth. Closer to getting Anna back.

Alexa refocused on her laptop. Code flashed across the screen. Scrolling green numbers and letters. All illegible to me.

"I still think Renaud is behind all of this." I brought my forehead to my hand, memories from the last few months resurfacing. "I don't trust the prick. I feel like he's at the center of everything somehow."

What if Anna and I hadn't canceled our wedding the first time? Would she be safe now?

Was this all my fault?

"Ma's calling." I looked over at Holly now sitting back on the bed with her mobile clutched in her palm. "Do I answer?"

"Maybe we wait until we have better news," I said, hating that I couldn't be there for my mother when she was probably losing her mind with Anna being gone and now our father being arrested.

My brothers had messaged me on my way to the hotel they were going to the Garda station, as if they could actually talk some sense into the detectives.

No, whoever masterminded all of this had set us up like chess pieces, but like hell I'd let him call *checkmate.*

"Shit." Holly was on her feet, her eyes wide. "Ma texted." She showed me the mobile.

"What's wrong?" Alexa faced us.

"Ethan and Sean were in an accident." I immediately dialed Ma.

"Holly, are you with Adam?" she cried out.

"Yeah, we're together," Holly said. "What happened?"

"Some guy ran Ethan and Sean . . . off the road and . . . pushed their car right over the bridge," she rushed out between broken sobs. "They're okay. They got out of the car before it went under the water. But . . . what's going on?"

I looked at Alexa, and I knew her thoughts were a mirror of my own.

I needed to get Holly and Ma somewhere safe. And now.

CHAPTER TWELVE

ADAM

"JUST STAY WITH SECURITY AND DON'T LEAVE THE ROOM until this is over. You understand?"

Holly held her hands up between us. "And what about you? They could come after you, too."

I'd hired half the city to guard my family. I wouldn't let this sick son of a bitch get to them.

I probably should've done the same with Anna when Donovan had threatened her way back when, but I'd given in to my desire to fight.

But this was one fight I couldn't mess up. I had to save her, and the right way.

And I had to protect my family in the process.

"I'm not in danger." I flicked my wrist, waving her back into the room.

"If you're not, then why are you protecting the rest of us?"

"Don't you get it?" I placed a fist over my heart. "They already got to me. They took Anna, and that's worse than a thousand deaths." My voice strained with emotion, and I couldn't hide the waver in my tone as guilt plunged a knife in my heart. I couldn't help but feel responsible for her being taken.

"Someone wants revenge," she whispered. "Who would go to such lengths to hurt our family?" She braced a hand on the interior frame of the door. "It can't be someone from Donovan's past. This is way too planned out. Too—"

"Personal," I finished. "I have to go. Just promise me you'll stay in this room until we get Anna back."

"Renaud and that limo driver were both at the Garda station when you were there, right? So, it couldn't be them who ran them off the road."

"Yeah, I mean—the Garda may have let them go right away after Da's confession, but shit, I don't know." I was so confused about everything. I couldn't think clearly with Anna in danger.

"What if . . ." She shook her head, not wanting to finish her line of thought. And thank God, because I couldn't stomach offering an answer.

"This will be over soon. I promise." I turned before she could argue and headed to meet up with Alexa.

I was relieved to see Xander and Jake back.

"What do you know?" I asked once the door closed behind me.

"We spoke to Lenny Johnson. He's the one who invited Kate to Renaud's club. But he wasn't the same man who hit on Anna. That may have been random, or hell, he was also paid off to hit on Anna," Jake said.

"What do you mean 'also paid off'?"

"Turns out Lenny was offered five hundred euros to convince Kate to go to Renaud's that Friday," Alexa answered. "He got half the cash the night he first talked to Kate, and he'd get the other half if she actually showed."

I shook my head at his words, at the extent at which this

arsehole had planned out everything to get to my family. "What happened?"

"Lenny decided to pocket the two-fifty and never even went to Renaud's that Friday," she said.

"If it was Renaud who staged all of this, he wouldn't need to go to such lengths to get Callaghan there," Xander said.

"Unless he was trying to throw the trail off himself." I wasn't ready to let Renaud off the hook.

"Maybe." Doubt clung to the word when she'd spoken, though.

"Well, uh, did this Lenny guy say what the man looked like who paid him?" I asked. "And can we trust he's even telling the truth?"

Jake handed me a photo of Lenny. "He doesn't look like the man who left Anna's hotel room, but that doesn't mean he's not lying."

I stared at the image, nearly crumpling it. "What else did he say? Anything useful?"

"He claims the guy had short brown hair. Green eyes. About five-ten," Jake said. "We showed Lenny a hundred different images from the list you gave us of people Anna or you've encountered in the last few months."

"None matched?" I handed him back the photo.

"No," she replied. "Renaud said his driver saw someone give Callaghan an envelope outside the club, but if someone went to such lengths to ensure we caught Callaghan parked outside the entrance around when Anna showed—we would've seen the exchange of the blackmail on camera."

"And all we saw was Callaghan leaning against the limo as if he were waiting for someone," Xander added.

"So, who is lying? The driver?" I cursed under my breath. "I saw him at the station. He has brown hair, but hell, so does half of Dublin."

Alexa looked to Jake for a long beat before her eyes traveled back to mine. "My gut's telling me we're missing the big picture." She was on her feet now with folded arms. "I think we need to determine the abductor's connection to both your father and Callaghan."

"As far as I know, Renaud and my father never crossed paths until the station today. Are you thinking whoever took Anna already knew both Callaghan and my father?"

Shit. We needed the Garda to let us talk to Da, to find out what he knew about the son of a bitch who threatened him into confessing.

"I think this is personal for whoever took Anna," Jake said and stood next to Alexa. "He took your fiancée on your wedding day. And then he had your father arrested for murder. Your brothers were driven off the road."

"If he threatened Da into confessing, then why almost kill my brothers? Wouldn't he worry Da would tell the Garda the truth?" I asked, my pulse racing.

"It could've been our suspect's way of further scaring your father into silence," Xander said, and I turned to look at him.

"There's no one you know with the skills to pull all . . ." Alexa's words dropped at the sound of a pinging noise coming from her laptop. "Give me a second." She sat back at the desk and began working at the keys.

Jake looked over her shoulder. "Were you right?"

"Right about what?" I bit down on my back teeth and stepped closer.

"Callaghan was under investigation by the Fraud Squad at the location in Cork." She peered at me from over her shoulder. "AKA, the Garda National Economic Crime Bureau. There was an active investigation looking into him for racketeering and financial corruption, among other crimes."

"And what happened?" I swallowed.

"The case was closed on March first. Not enough evidence, but according to the lead detective, he believed Callaghan paid someone off to shut it down. His notes suggest Sebastian Renaud may have helped him out."

"Shit." My body tensed. "There's more, though, isn't there?"

She nodded. "Your father was being looked at, too. But the case was only open for two weeks before it was shut down."

"When?" I asked.

She focused on the screen again. "The case was opened on March seventeenth by Detective McCaffrey. Closed on April third."

"March seventeenth? That was a week after Da's heart attack." I rubbed at my forehead. "Who was the detective again?"

"Peter McCaffrey." She worked at her keys. "But, um . . ."

"What?" I crossed the short space between us to get a better view of her screen.

"McCaffrey was forced to take personal leave on April second."

"And my father's case was closed the next day?" That couldn't be a coincidence.

"Yeah." Alexa stood again and turned toward us, and I could tell by the hard look in her eyes she figured something out. "But I think I know what happened."

I couldn't take this. I was on the verge of a heart attack myself. "What?"

She let go of a breath. "There was a car accident. And

well, I'm pretty sure McCaffrey blames your father for his wife and daughter's deaths."

* * *

"I STILL CAN'T BELIEVE I WAS NEAR THIS MOTHERFUCKER today." I stared at the screen, unable to process the fact I'd been meters away from McCaffrey, so close to the man who had Anna.

I'd been hell-bent on wanting to blame Renaud, and McCaffrey had walked right past me at the Garda station.

I wanted to kill the son of a bitch.

"Why the hell are the Garda taking so long to get back to us about this new lead?" I looked at Jake and Xander who were gearing up as if ready for an attack.

I hated this. Hated every fecking thing about it.

"You any closer to triangulating a position from the calls and messages McCaffrey made to Callaghan? If he's at that location now, Anna will hopefully be there, too." Jake strapped a gun near his ankle, and then he hid it with his cargo pants.

"I've got it narrowed down, but the search area is still too wide," she replied.

Of all people, we were dealing with a detective who specialized in economic and cybercrimes. I still couldn't wrap my head around the fact a detective had been posing as one of Renaud's limo drivers. And it'd been him to supply Callaghan with the blackmail, using Lenny, among others, to throw us off his tracks.

"Are we sure Renaud's not part of this as opposed to another tool used by McCaffrey?" I asked.

"Someone like Renaud would have nothing to gain and

everything to lose," she began. "Renaud runs an empire—he's not exactly responsible for hiring his drivers and such."

She took a moment to let me digest the information.

"His assistant said Renaud isn't the easiest man to work for, and so, she was constantly dealing with a rotating door of employees," she added.

"And the assistant didn't find it odd when Callaghan personally requested this new driver—McCaffrey—for his trip this time to Dublin?" Jake asked.

"Apparently not," Alexa answered.

"So, McCaffrey loses his wife and daughter in a car accident, and then immediately goes back to work that Monday?" *Who the hell does that?* "And then uses his resources at his job to try and figure out who was to blame for the accident?"

No way did Da run McCaffrey's family off the road and just drive away.

No damn way.

"The guy became unhinged when he lost his family. He had one mission in mind: revenge," Jake said for the second time in the last twenty minutes, repeating his words since nothing seemed to be sticking with me.

I was beginning to lose it. Hell, maybe I already had lost it.

"Just because Da was driving a similar vehicle within a few kilometers of where McCaffrey said the accident happened, doesn't make Da a murderer." I gritted my teeth.

"I agree, but he clearly needed someone to blame," Alexa said softly. "And within a few days of being back at work, he launched the bogus racketeering case against your father as a way to get the court-ordered surveillance to help enact his plans."

"But then he was forced to take personal leave," Jake said.

"Which maybe, if they'd done from the beginning, none of this would've happened," she replied.

"McCaffrey had already been investigating Callaghan and was pissed the case got closed. He knew everything about the man, which was how he knew to target Renaud as his way in to get to Callaghan," she explained. "Since Callaghan's predictable and always uses Renaud's hotels, drivers, and so forth—it'd be the logical choice for McCaffrey."

"Plus, he blamed Renaud for making the Callaghan case go away," Xander added. "McCaffrey may even have plans for Renaud, too."

I closed my eyes, a memory rising to the surface and guilt came with it.

My fingertips went to my eyes, and I applied pressure there, seeing little dots. "The Garda questioned Da about his whereabouts the night of his heart attack right after surgery since he owned a red Lamborghini. I vaguely remembered hearing about that accident on the news, too." *A lone survivor of a tragedy. Peter McCaffrey, a resident of Cork* . . . "That's why the limo driver looked familiar to me at the station. I'd seen his face on the news." I cursed under my breath. "It's a strong motive, and it didn't come to mind."

"No, man, don't blame yourself," Jake said. "We're going to get her back and alive. I wouldn't be prepping for a rescue if I didn't believe that."

"Yeah," I said under my breath. "But what if Anna's already dead?" I didn't want to think those words, let alone say them, but it was a possible truth. The ugliest truth imaginable.

McCaffrey was out for blood. Vengeance. And he'd

planned an elaborate scheme to destroy my family since he believed my father got away with murder.

"We already know he's capable of killing," I said, thinking about Callaghan.

"And now that we know McCaffrey's also such a heartless bastard since he investigated his own brother-in-law and put him in—"

"The brother-in-law!" Alexa cut off Jake. "Shit. McCaffrey doesn't have a place in Dublin, but the brother-in-law does. His home is just outside the city. It'd be empty since he's in prison."

"Where's it at?" Jake stood behind her as she zoomed in on a map.

"Two kilometers from one of the cell towers we got a hit on from a text sent to Callaghan." She pointed at the screen. "I think Anna's there."

CHAPTER THIRTEEN

ANNA

"You can't do it, can you?" I tugged at the zip ties pinning my wrists to the headboard of the bed. A waste of effort. "You can't kill me."

My legs weren't tied down, but my wrists ached from rubbing against the plastic as I fought to get free over and over again.

"You're a means to an end." He was pacing alongside the bed, gun in hand.

I'd barely been in the same room with him all day, thank God, but I was pretty sure I now knew why.

"The woman in the photo with that man—she's someone special to you, right?"

He stopped walking and averted his eyes toward the picture of a man with his arm draped over the shoulder of a blonde woman at his side. "Don't talk about my wife," he hissed and rubbed the butt of the gun to his forehead. His right arm flexed, the muscle straining against the fabric of his white sleeve.

"I look like her." His wife had the same hair as me. The same green eyes. Even bone structure.

I wasn't sure what he'd been doing all day, and honestly, I didn't want to know, but I had to find a way to keep myself alive. To talk myself out of this. At least, to buy time until Adam could get to me. Because he would find me. I knew it. He always came through.

I had to believe everything would be okay.

I loved Adam so much, and so this couldn't be it for us. We'd been through too much for it to end on a day we were supposed to say our vows.

"You don't have to be a killer."

"I believe in justice." He turned and faced me, his eyes thinning as he observed me.

"But what'd I do to you? What'd I do to deserve this?" I tried to fight the tremble in my tone.

He edged closer to the bed and cocked his head. "I've always played by the rules." His voice was low and deep. "My brother-in-law," he began while pointing the muzzle of the gun toward the picture on the wall, "was no exception." He lightly shook his head. "He committed fraud, and so, I was the first to lead the investigation and make the arrest."

Oh, God.

"The guilty must be punished."

"But what am I guilty of?" I lifted my chin, pinning my eyes to his.

He lowered his arm, gun still in hand, and kept his face pointed my way. "You know how many rich arseholes I've witnessed buying themselves out of trouble?" He tsked. "No justice. No punishment."

I had no idea what the hell he was talking about, but as long as I kept him talking, I didn't give a damn.

My gaze veered to the open doorway, clinging to the hope Adam would somehow appear—that if I focused on the visual of him arriving hard enough, it'd happen.

His jaw clenched. "I'm tired of it. Tired of the very system I work for letting these criminals go." His eyes thinned. "But McGregor—he stole everything from me. My wife. Daughter. Job."

"What?" I sucked in sharp breaths, my chest hurting from such deep inhalations. "Adam would never . . ."

"Adam's father killed them," he bit back.

Killed? My stomach tucked in at his words. At his grief-stricken motive for taking me.

"His sons are no better." He took a step away from the bed and arched his shoulders back before cracking his neck from side to side. "They'll become like him if I let it happen."

"I don't understand," I sputtered.

"And why would you?" He started pacing again. "You're marrying one of them. Well, you were going to."

"I don't know what happened, but you don't have to do this." Any last thread of strength I'd been clinging to was starting to slip, realizing death was imminent. "Please," I tried one more time.

"No." He faced me. "You have to die. McGregor has to suffer for what he did. He needs to rot in prison while I take everything from him, starting with taking his favorite son's fiancée." He clicked off the safety and raised his arm.

I squeezed my eyes closed, but after moments of silence, I looked to find the gun at his side.

Had he changed his mind?

Hope climbed inside of me, but then a gut-wrenchingly bad feeling hit my stomach as he eyed his watch before snatching the photo of his wife off the wall.

"I can't shoot you, you're right." He came closer to the bed with the gun in one hand and photo in the other. "But that was never the plan."

I wasn't sure what the hell the psycho was talking about,

but it didn't matter, because I caught sight of a flutter of movement outside the door. A shadow? Maybe my eyes were playing tricks on me.

No! I screamed on the inside when the guy whirled around to follow my gaze—and Adam appeared at that exact moment.

I barely had time to grapple with the fact Adam was there because now both men faced each other with guns drawn.

Terror filled my lungs, making it hard to breathe as I observed the scene. If Adam died trying to save me . . . "Please," I cried. "Don't."

Adam's blue eyes found mine for only a second before he focused on my captor and stepped into the room.

"Put the gun down." His voice was a rough command; his tone clipped but confident.

He had to have backup; he'd never come alone and risk something going sideways.

But I also knew it couldn't be the police because no way would they let Adam handle this moment.

"The Garda are on their way, McCaffrey," Adam said. "It's over."

McCaffrey? God, my captor had a name now.

"You're not supposed to be here." The man shook his head. "This isn't how it's supposed to happen."

"I guess you're not as smart as you think," Adam rasped.

"Your father killed my wife and daughter. We were here on vacation, and the bastard ran us off the road and didn't even stop to help!"

"You don't know for certain it was him. The police closed the investigation about the accident," Adam said, his voice low and calm. He was somehow keeping it together, maintaining control of the situation. "Maybe if you hadn't rushed back to work so soon after your family died, you wouldn't have jumped to conclusions."

"Fuck you!" he roared. "You. Your father. Your deep pockets. Of course, the Garda closed the case. You don't think your old man paid them off? But I looked at his medical records. He'd been drinking that night. I caught his vehicle on the traffic cams in Dublin leaving the city shortly before the accident. The timing works out too perfectly for it not to be him."

"If my father's responsible he'll be punished." Adam's eyes briefly connected with mine.

"No. He got away with it already. I won't let him get away with it again."

"Put the gun down. The only one who will die today is you if you don't."

My heart was a permanent fixture in my throat. Emotion strangling my breath.

"I'll put it down if you do, and we can settle this the way you know best," McCaffrey suggested in an eerily calm voice. "With our fists."

Adam was the best fighter I'd ever seen, but this guy was also very jacked and hell-bent on vengeance.

"We don't have time. You and I both know that."

"So, you found the explosives?"

Explosives? "Get out of here, Adam," I cried in a panic.

"You must have more people with you. I guess they're preoccupied right now." He continued to hold on tight to the photo in his free hand as he focused on Adam. "Since you know we're down to a few minutes, we better make this quick. We lose our weapons at the same time."

I could see the sweat on Adam's brow, the movement in his throat.

But . . . he had people with him, and those people would diffuse the bombs. They had to.

"Fine." Adam waited for McCaffrey to crouch, and then he followed suit. Adam must've realized the safest option for everyone was to get rid of the weapons.

We'll be okay, I told myself, needing to believe it.

I squeezed my eyes closed, not able to watch what would happen next.

But at the sound of a fist connecting to flesh a moment later, I opened my eyes.

The guns were on the floor now and off to the sides, and McCaffrey stood before Adam, swiping his fists in the air.

One landed on Adam's jaw, but the next missed.

Adam ducked another wild swing, then pounded his clenched hand into the man's ribs.

My heartbeat worked harder and faster, and I shook my wrists, trying to fight the zip ties again, ignoring the plastic cutting into my skin.

The guy attempted to plow round after round Adam's way, but Adam deflected every punch. And every kick.

It was as if Adam was letting him make all the moves, allowing the guy to wear himself out.

McCaffrey was big. Strong and built.

Adam was toned and lithe, and he could last much longer. He was saving his energy for the right moment. He was making calculated moves.

And then, Adam's signature hard left punch slammed into his cheek.

It was clear McCaffrey was trying to remain standing, but he looked wobbly. He fell to his knees and dropped forward.

Was it over?

It felt like horse hooves were on top of my chest, and I couldn't gather in a deep breath.

The room was closing in on me, and if I wasn't already on a bed, I probably would've fainted.

How much time did we have left?

Adam stepped over him to get to me, but then I saw a flash of movement.

McCaffrey was already on his feet.

"Adam!" I screamed, but it was too late.

He'd grabbed his gun and swung it hard, knocking the butt of the weapon against Adam's temple.

Adam lost his balance, and his palms landed on the bed.

He was so close to me, and yet, he felt so damn far.

"Adam," I cried, tears now trailing lines down my cheeks as his eyes met mine.

He blinked a few times, then shifted toward him so fast I almost missed it. He wrapped his hands around McCaffrey's arms, forcing the gun to point in the air and away from me.

"Drop it!" an unfamiliar voice roared from somewhere in the room, but I couldn't take my eyes off Adam.

Adam used the weight of his body to push him across the room and up against the wall and gasping breaths left McCaffrey as he struggled with Adam.

My shoulders shook at the sound of a gunshot, a sound I remembered from watching my father shoot his shotgun back in Kentucky.

The bullet penetrated the ceiling as Adam continued to keep the guy's arms up in the air.

I swung my gaze over to two strangers now in the room, both with guns drawn. If they were here, it had to mean the place wasn't going to blow up. But damnit, there was still a gun way too close to Adam.

One of the men, a guy with warm brown eyes, looked at me and lightly nodded as if he were telling me everything would be okay.

The strangers didn't have a clear shot at McCaffrey, though, since Adam had him pinned to the wall.

Blood trickled down the side of Adam's neck, but he seemed unfazed by whatever damage to his skull had occurred when McCaffrey hit him.

Adam brought his knee toward the guy over and over again, but the damn man wouldn't relent.

And then Adam shifted his head back slightly before knocking his forehead hard against his.

I couldn't see McCaffrey's face, but Adam did it two more times, and then McCaffrey lost hold of his gun and started to slide down the wall.

Adam faced the room and moved toward me as if nothing in the world could keep him away. "Anna," he whispered.

I gasped at the sight of Adam as he shook his head, opening and closing his eyes a few times as blood from a cut on his forehead hit his eyelashes.

"Oh, God. Are you okay?"

He sat next to me and anchored his palms on my cheeks. "Me?" He found my eyes without losing hold of my face. "Are *you* okay?"

"Yeah," I whispered.

"The explosives have been deactivated," someone said a moment later. "We swept the rest of the house and property to be certain there weren't any more. Found another, which was why it took us so long to get to you."

I forced my attention away from Adam to see the stranger handing him a knife. Adam freed my hands and pulled me tight against him.

"You're hurt," I cried against his chest.

"I'm . . . fine," he said, his voice breaking. "I'm just so glad you're okay. I'm so damn sorry." He stood and lifted me into his arms, and it was then that I heard sirens wailing in the distance. "I'm gonna kill Da," he said under his breath as we left the room.

* * *

"I DON'T NEED TO BE IN A HOSPITAL." I WASN'T THE ONE WHO got hurt.

"There were bombs, Anna," my dad said in a low, gravelly voice. "What was Adam thinking charging into that home with two civilians?"

"And if he hadn't, our baby girl would be dead!" my mom came to Adam's defense before I had a chance to say anything. She held my hand tight between her palms, tears still gliding down her cheeks like they had been since I'd arrived there an hour ago.

"This isn't the kind of life I want for you." My dad rubbed his forehead, and I was pretty sure he'd aged ten years since yesterday. "A detective kidnapped you, Anna!" He cursed. "A detective!"

"She doesn't need this right now," my sister, Dana, said from where she sat in the row of chairs in front of the window, alongside Becca and Sheri.

I glanced at Holly who was standing next to where my mom sat. A nervous energy hit me when our eyes connected. "How are Ethan and Sean?"

"They'll be okay." Holly forced a small smile. "They're relieved to hear you're back and that you and Adam are also okay."

"Thank God." Relief struck me. "Uh, how long will Adam be at the police station?"

"He texted me he'll be leaving with Da soon," she replied.

"According to those reporters outside the hospital—your

family is responsible for everything that happened." The angry bite of my father's words had my stomach protesting.

"I'm . . ." Holly seized a breath of air and released it. "I'm truly sorry for what happened."

"You don't need to apologize," I said, knowing today could've turned out much differently.

One man had died, and many others could've as well.

I still couldn't quite grasp what had happened, or how I'd managed not to completely break down during it all. Then again, I was in love with a man who made me feel like the strongest woman in the world, and so . . .

"Peter McCaffrey lost his family, and he misplaced his rage onto yours," my mother finished for me when the words became stuck in my throat. At least she didn't blame Adam's family for everything the way my dad now did.

"Who were those men with Adam?"

"Oh, um." Holly strode closer to the bed, and my mom scooted her chair to the side a little, but never lost hold of my hand. I was beginning to think she'd never let go. "Adam hired them to find you. Marco recommended them. Supposedly the best of the best at tracking people down."

"Maybe you should consider coming back home after everything that's happened." Dad's words had my gaze winging to the other side of the bed to catch his eyes.

I shook my head. "I am home."

CHAPTER FOURTEEN

ADAM

"THE MURDER CHARGES HAVE BEEN DROPPED, BUT GIVEN THE lengths to which McCaffrey went to punish your father, we're going to reopen the case about the car accident. To make sure McCaffrey wasn't telling the truth about your father."

If it was truly Da who ran McCaffrey's family off the road, resulting in their deaths, then my father deserved whatever punishment he got.

I pressed the heel of my palm to my forehead where a bandage covered the wound. If Anna had gotten shot . . .

She's okay, I reminded myself, so I didn't lose it.

"I'm sorry we didn't piece all of this together, but you should also never have gone to get her without us. I gave you orders to stand down and wait for us to get there."

"And if we waited she would've died!" I dropped my hand from my face. "The psycho wired the place with fecking explosives. He was minutes from blowing her up."

A million curses hung on the tip of my tongue.

"You're lucky you had ex-agents with you, or things could've gone much differently."

Jake and Xander had denied my request to take point, but

when we showed up, they had no choice but to let me save Anna so they could deactivate the devices.

"And if you'd worked faster after I tipped you off about McCaffrey being the limo driver—we could've gotten to Anna sooner." I shook my head, my blood heating.

He quietly observed me, but he knew I was right. "Go get stitches," he sputtered after a moment. "You look like hell." He turned and left.

Once I caught sight of Da being discharged from the room behind where I stood, I left the station and headed for where I parked my Audi.

The buzz of questions filled the air from reporters once outside, but I pushed through, never looking back to check if Da was there.

Of course, I didn't need to look.

I could feel him. The burn of shame blowing in the wind and hitting me hard.

Was it really possible McCaffrey had been right about the accident? He'd been right about Brian Callaghan; the bastard had been a criminal, and he'd taken the blackmail without any second thoughts.

Of course, Callaghan had no clue he'd been spoon-fed the blackmail by the same man who'd led the investigation against him for criminal charges a few months back.

"Talk," I said once we were both inside the vehicle, and I continued to ignore the lights from cameras clicking outside the Audi.

They were a hazy blur to me right now.

Da scratched at his chin before covering his mouth, and my eyes lingered on the white mark around his finger. He hadn't put his wedding band back on after the Garda had returned his belongings.

Ma had stayed at the hospital with my brothers. She'd

probably surrendered to the notion Da was guilty. Maybe I had as well.

"Adam."

"Shit. This isn't right." I waved my hand in the air. "Let's not do this with the media just outside."

I caught a nod out of my peripheral view, and I peeled away from the curb.

After a few minutes, I pulled off to the side of the road and killed the engine.

"I'm so damn sorry. If anything happened to you kids . . ." He reached for me, but I swatted his arm away, too bloody pissed and in need of answers. "I didn't kill anyone, Son." His tanned throat moved with a hard swallow. "I promise. The first time I ever set eyes on Peter McCaffrey was in Callaghan's hotel room."

"But you were questioned about the accident. I remember. There's only a few red Lamborghinis in the city, and—"

"I *was* driving that night, but I didn't run anyone off the road. And when I got home, I had the heart attack." He held a palm in the air between us, as if giving me his solemn word.

A tightness stretched across my chest, and I rubbed at the achiness there. Could I believe him?

"Did you know McCaffrey was investigating you? Our company?" I thought back to what we'd discovered. Well, what Alexa had found out about McCaffrey.

"No, I had no idea. But I assume that's how he got the photos."

"The blackmail?" I dropped my hands to my lap and looked back at him.

"He had me followed. Got pictures of me spending time with another woman." He sighed as if his words were more of an inconvenience than a blow to the left cheek. "I would never have sold MAC for so cheap to Callaghan because of those photos, but I verbally agreed to the sale to buy myself some time to handle the situation until after your wedding." His eyes appeared pale. Hollow. A fraction of the titan businessman he once was. "Callaghan was going to have the photos published today, and I didn't want to ruin your wedding for a second time."

My stomach knotted. "You were having an affair?" The question came out as a whisper of disbelief.

My father had been a lot of things, but a cheater had never been one of them. At least, I hadn't thought so. But was cheating better than murdering a mom and her eight-year-old daughter? Yeah.

"No, there was no affair. I didn't . . ." He rubbed a hand over his dry lips. "Your mom and I are separated, but we didn't want anyone to know. The company had gone public, and you were planning your wedding. Plus, my heart attack delayed your wedding the first time. I didn't want to ruin everything again."

His words plucked the air right out of the car, and I squeezed the skin at my throat as if I were suffocating.

"We planned to tell you kids a few weeks after your wedding. It didn't feel like the right time."

"I don't understand." My world—everything I thought I knew about my parents—felt as if it were spinning. Rotating the wrong fecking way.

"McCaffrey told me he'd kill Anna and destroy our family if I didn't confess to the murder." His lids dropped, hiding his eyes from view. "I'm so sorry about everything, but I promise I had nothing to do with his wife and daughter dying. He needed someone to blame, and clearly, he set his sights on me. And that's the God's honest truth."

I wanted to believe him, but I wasn't sure if I could.

With McCaffrey behind bars, all I wanted to do was be with Anna.

She was back and safe.

And so maybe I'd wait to decide whether Da was a liar and a murderer.

CHAPTER FIFTEEN

ADAM

HER FINGERS LIGHTLY FEATHERED OVER THE GAUZE TAPED TO my forehead; her lips were downturned. "I hate that you got hurt."

"You're okay, so I'm okay. If anything had happened to you . . ."

"Don't think like that." Tears welled in her eyes. "I love you so much."

I swallowed the lump of emotion down my throat. "You sure you still want to marry into my family?"

"Yes, I—" She let go of her words at the sound of the door buzzer.

"Stay here. I'll be right back." I pulled on a shirt and left the bedroom to see who was outside our flat.

I checked the outdoor cameras and relief struck me at the sight of Alexa, Jake, and Xander standing outside.

I'd been high-strung for the last two days since Anna had come home from the hospital. We'd barricaded ourselves inside to hide from the press, and so I could keep her all to myself.

And most of our friends and family who'd flown in for

the wedding had already left Dublin. We'd had to issue yet another rain check. But to hell with everything, I was going to marry Anna no matter what, and if the universe was trying to stop me—good luck with that.

"Hey, sorry to show up like this," Jake had said when I let them in a minute later. "You didn't answer your phone."

I scrubbed a hand down my scratchy beard. "Sorry, I've been avoiding calls. Had it turned off."

"I don't blame you," Alexa said, and her attention wandered over my shoulder, and I turned to see Anna padding our way in sweats and a loose-fitting black tee. *My* tee.

"Hi," Anna said.

"How are you holding up?" Xander asked as I motioned for everyone to have a seat.

"Okay, thanks to you all." Anna sat next to me and slipped her hand inside of mine. "I really can't thank you enough."

The team had visited Anna before, but I wasn't sure if we'd ever grow tired of thanking them. I owed them everything.

"Well, we're about to head back to London, but we had some news to share with you first," Jake said, his brown eyes lifting to meet mine from where he sat.

I leaned forward, nervous as to what he was about to lay on me.

"Thirty minutes ago, we handed over information to the Garda about the car accident." Jake looked at Alexa next to him for a brief moment before redirecting his focus back on me.

Anna squeezed my hand, offering the support she knew I needed.

"Peter McCaffrey was right about the red Lamborghini, but he was wrong about the driver."

I bowed my head.

"One of the owners of the vehicle who'd been questioned had an alibi. He and his wife were out of town," Alexa started. "But his sixteen-year-old kid had been home. In his original statement, he denied driving the vehicle."

"But it was him?" My lungs filled from a deep breath.

"He'd been scared," Alexa said. "There's a sharp bend in the road where the accident occurred. He was coming from the other direction too fast and had crossed over into the other lane. He corrected his car to prevent a collision, but it was too late. McCaffrey had jerked his vehicle too hard, and he went off the road."

"What'd the kid do after?" Anna asked.

"He was afraid of getting in trouble, and so he made an anonymous call to the police about the accident and took off."

I was on my feet at his words, and I moved over to the wall of windows and pressed a palm to the glass.

A mom and daughter had tragically died, but it wasn't because of Da.

At the feel of Anna's hand on my back, I drew in a deep breath and slowly let it out, allowing a sense of calm to take over me.

"McCaffrey chose the wrong man to come after," Jake said.

I turned to face him, threading my fingers with Anna's again. "Thank you so much." I stepped closer to the team, who were now all standing, and brought Anna with me, our hands still united. "For everything," I said, emotion settling like a lump in my throat.

Anna left my side to hug Alexa, and then Xander and Jake.

We said our goodbyes, and after I locked up, I faced my fiancée, and a line etched between her brows as she eyed me. "How about no more wedding planning? Can we just run away and get married?"

I crossed the room and gathered her in my arms, relieved the nightmare was over.

"You're sure you—"

She pressed a finger to my lips, silencing me. Her beautiful green eyes grew damp. "I know with your parents' separation maybe you don't want to get married right now, but . . ." She allowed her words to fade as she stepped out of my embrace.

"They're not us," I whispered. "And nothing could stop me from wanting to be your husband."

Her lips curved into a slight smile. "Then yes, I want to marry you, and as soon as possible."

I nipped her bottom lip and nuzzled my nose against hers. "Then I think I have an idea."

CHAPTER SIXTEEN

HOLLY

"I DON'T KNOW HOW YOU EVEN GOT TO THIS FLOOR, BUT you're not allowed to see Monsieur Renaud."

"I don't care if he's the king of France. I want to see him. Now!"

"We don't have a king anymore," the woman bit back. "I'm calling security."

"I came all the way to Paris to talk to him, and that's exactly what I'm going to do!" I glared at the woman as she stood in front of Renaud's door trying to block me from going inside.

The woman nearly fell backward when Renaud opened the door, and he grabbed hold of her elbow to help her remain upright. "I'm so sorry, Monsieur Renaud. I tried to get her to leave."

His dark eyes pinned to mine, even though he was holding onto his admin. "I heard you," he said before pulling his attention from me to her. "Why don't you get us something to drink?"

She repositioned herself to look at Renaud, and although I

couldn't see her face, I was betting there was a major glare or jaw-drop moment happening.

"Now." He stepped back, and she began cursing in French under her breath before she strode away, her heels clicking angrily on the tile as she left.

I dropped my bag onto the couch in front of his desk and moved over to the window to view the Eiffel Tower in the distance, shining like a beacon beneath the rays of the sun.

When I pivoted to face him, his hands were tucked into his gray trouser pockets with his back to his desk.

I tensed as his gaze raked over the length of my body, starting at my nude heels, before gliding up over my bare legs and to the hem of my black pencil skirt. His eyes settled on mine after briefly viewing my white blouse.

My skin warmed beneath his stare. This was becoming the norm every time we were in the same room.

But damnit, I was mad at him. And I didn't want to feel anything other than anger.

"Why'd you buy our stock?" I asked while closing the gap between us so I could stand close to him.

Shit, we were too close. His smell wafted to my nose, and I did my best not to take in a deep breath.

"Your stock prices were going through the floor after everything that happened, and I saw it as an opportunity to invest." His dark brows arched as he continued to hold my eyes.

"You bought up so much stock you now have a seat on our board," I yelled, my hands flailing like a crazy person, nearly whacking him in the chest in the process since we were so close to each other.

He tipped his head to the side and continued to observe me, almost as if he were amused by my state.

"Adam doesn't trust you after everything that happened with your limo driver and—"

"How could I know it was him?"

"Maybe if you weren't such an arrogant jerk you could keep your employees around a little bit longer?" This time, I did touch him. I pressed down his gray tie to the crisp black dress shirt. "Did you pay someone off to help get the case closed on Callaghan? Is that why he owed you a favor?" I had to know the truth. I had to know if he was somehow, in part, to blame for everything that'd happened.

"Why does it matter?"

He leaned in closer, and my palm flattened on the hard wall of his chest.

The muscles . . .

I blinked, trying to regroup and maintain my focus.

I'd come all the way to Paris to yell at him, to try and get him to sell the stock back, and here I was, preoccupied with the look in his eyes and the way he made me feel.

"I have to know."

"Three years ago, I gave him a loan to prevent his company from going under. That's it." His voice was deep, rich, and the huskiness had me lifting my hand free and staggering back a step. "Whether you believe me or not, that's up to you."

I processed his words, but I honestly had no idea what to think.

"You need to sell. I can't have you on the board." I shook my head. "I can't work with you. See you all of the time." I opened my palms in the air. "You have this place. You have offices in London. Your many businesses in Dublin. What do you need with my company?"

"Your company needed help after your family name was dragged through the mud. And had I not bought the stock—"

"No," I rasped. "Don't act like you did us a favor." I faked a laugh. "And I swear, if you tell me I owe you something in return for this help, I'll lose my bloody mind."

His lips tugged at the edges like he was trying to subdue a smile. He lifted his hands from his pockets and pressed the heels of his hands on each side of the desk.

"What do you find so funny?"

He slowly traced a line over his bottom lip with his tongue, as if contemplating the things he wanted to do with it to me.

I was about to become liquid if I stayed in his presence any longer.

How could I ever work with this man?

No, I couldn't let it happen.

"You're fairly put-together. A strong woman." He pushed away from the desk to stand before me. "So, why is it whenever you're around me you blush like this?" He cupped my right cheek, and his thumb swept in little circular movements as he held my eyes captive.

I was locked in place. Unable to move. To breathe. To think a coherent thought.

Never in my life had I felt like this before, and I didn't want to feel like this again, which was why I had to get him to back off from McGregor Enterprises.

Da hadn't killed anyone.

Anna was safe.

And if it weren't for the media spreading so many rumors the company wouldn't have been put in such a weak state.

Maybe we never should have taken the company public, opening our doors to a vulture like him.

"Sell your stock."

He released his hold of me. "No."

I hung my head and gripped my temples, trying to figure a way out of this situation.

"But while you're in Paris, I could recommend a few places to eat so this trip isn't a total waste of your time." He went around to his desk, and at the sound of a knock, he replied to it with a, "Never mind. Miss McGregor was just leaving."

The door never opened, and I assumed his admin was relieved to hear the news since she seemed to hate me on sight.

I snatched my bag from where I'd dropped it and started for the door.

"You don't want that list of restaurants?"

I halted and peeked at him from over my shoulder, observing him now seated at his desk. "No. You know exactly what I want." And yet, I could feel red rise up my throat at my words, especially when a grin touched his lips.

"I'm beginning to think I do."

CHAPTER SEVENTEEN

ANNA

"THIS WAS MY WEDDING GIFT TO YOU, BUT NOW I THINK IT'S the perfect place to get married."

My fingers combed through the hair of the dappled-gray Arabian mare in total shock. "These horses . . . this stable? It's really ours?" I bit into my lip and glimpsed Adam out of the corner of my eye.

"Instead of traveling an hour to ride, I thought you could have a place close to our new home." He gently gripped my bicep, urging me to face him, and I dropped my hand from the beautiful mare and steadied my eyes on Adam's.

"I don't even have words for this." My eyes became damp.

The kids at the McGregor Foundation we worked with would love it. "What'd I do to deserve such an incredible man?" I hooked my arms around his neck.

"I ask myself the same question every day about you." His lips split into a grin. "So, what do you think? You want to get married here and ride away on horses after we say *I do*?"

I'd joked about this before, and he'd remembered. Of

course, he'd remember. And, to be honest, it hadn't been that much of a joke. It was what felt right.

"More than anything. Yes."

He reached for my hand as we walked outside, and I stared at the greenery with the water shimmering in the distance.

It was my very own slice of heaven.

"I love you, Adam McGregor." His mouth captured mine, stealing my breath, my thoughts, my everything. "Make love to me," I said after a moment and looked around at the open field.

We were alone beneath a clear sky on a warm day.

"You don't want to wait until the wedding this weekend?" He raised a brow.

"We can pull it off that fast?" I asked in disbelief.

Four weeks ago, a man had kidnapped me and nearly blown Adam and me to pieces, and now . . . here I was, happier than I ever thought possible.

"It's already been arranged, and thank God you like the idea," he said with a smile.

I bit my lip as I studied the scar above his eye from his fight with Peter McCaffrey. "Well, in that case, I still don't want to wait. It's been weeks, and I want nothing more than to be with you." I pointed to the ground. "Right here. Right now."

He looked at my cowboy boots, the ones he'd asked me to wear before blindfolding me to take me on a drive to this place.

"Hell, yes." He gathered my face in his hands and kissed me hard, his tongue threading with mine, and I worked at his belt buckle, too eager to wait.

"Let me grab something," he murmured, then fled from my side.

I watched as he ran to his Audi parked a few hundred feet away, and I lifted my chin and closed my eyes, allowing the sun to wash over me.

"Here," he said when he returned, and I opened my eyes to find him spreading a heavy-duty quilt over the lush green grass.

My hands went to my hips as he stood. "You knew this would happen, huh?"

He lifted his shoulders and shot me an innocent smile. "A guy can't ever be too prepared, can he?" he asked, then wrestled me to the ground as I laughed.

CHAPTER EIGHTEEN

ANNA

Simple but elegant. And so utterly perfect.

Adam pulled me into his arms, his mouth slanted over mine, and his tongue caressed my lips right after we were proclaimed husband and wife.

The small crowd of people we'd invited roared with applause once our lips had separated, and we faced them.

Adam walked me down the aisle, hand in hand, and toward the white mares awaiting us.

We were truly going to ride off in the sunset.

I'd sketched this moment in my diary when I was a kid maybe five dozen times. All with different actors I'd been obsessed with growing up. You know the ones . . . the guys who'd adorned every magazine and had been in all the blockbuster movies.

But never for a moment did I actually believe this moment would come true, or that the man I'd marry would far surpass any childhood dreams.

I was Mrs. McGregor. I was Adam's forever.

He helped me onto my horse, and I shifted the sweeping

train of my dress off to the side and clutched the reins, even though I hadn't wanted to let go of him.

The cheers from behind continued as we rode, and the photographer snapped photos of us.

But it wasn't until the reception an hour later, and I was dancing with my father, that it really, truly hit me.

I was married.

"I was wrong about him, wasn't I?" Dad whispered in my ear as we danced. "He's a good man."

I fought to keep the tears at bay, knowing my waterproof mascara had already been tested far too many times. "Yes, he is." I rested my chin on his shoulder, stealing a glimpse of Adam with his hands tucked in his pockets watching us, his lip wedged between his teeth. "I love you, Dad," I said before we parted.

Dad shook Adam's hand and gave a firm nod before Adam gathered me into his arms to dance.

"I think he's finally coming around to you." My eyes roamed over the slim fit of his tux his broad shoulders filled out.

Adam in a bow tie was entirely too sexy to put into words.

"Well, that's a relief." I could hear the smile in his voice. "Did I tell you how amazing you look?"

I chuckled. "Only a hundred times."

I was wearing Adam's mother's dress since my older sister, Becca, had worn my mom's gown.

This one was stunning. Long and flowy with a sweetheart neckline. The dress tapered at the waist, and it had a romantic and breezy skirt embellished with light touches of lace.

I caught sight of his parents from over his shoulder as we danced. They were sitting together at a table on the edge of the makeshift dance floor beneath the white tent.

It was a romantic setting to fall back in love.

Adam's mom reached for her husband's hand, covering his with her palm, and the gesture had me swallowing.

Just maybe they'd work things out . . .

I gathered a breath, trying to stifle my emotions, and allowed my gaze to wander as Adam held me, soaking in everything about our location.

The tables were covered in white linen with handcrafted wooden chairs accompanying them. Amber yellow and warm red flowers were placed strategically around the tent, as well as within the center vases.

Strings of lights twinkled above and wrapped up a few of the poles that held up the tent. And garlands crisscrossed the pitched ceiling, giving an earthier and warmer feel.

"I think I owe you big-time for this." I pulled back to find his eyes.

"I won't ask for much, I swear." He winked. "Maybe a few babies. Four or five."

I tipped my head back and laughed. We were both from a family of four, so it was possible.

"I really love you, Mrs. McGregor."

"Mm. I love you, too."

"Tonight," he growled in my ear. "You're mine."

I shifted my long, wavy hair over my shoulder, and I could feel my nipples strain against the fabric at his words, despite the corset.

The memory of us making love together in the field just outside the tent earlier that week blew back to mind, and I suddenly had the desire to bail on our party so we could be alone.

"The babies you two will make . . ." Maggie, Marco's wife, said as she danced with Marco alongside us. "You're a stunning couple."

Like me, Maggie had left America and found love in another country. I'd grown to love her almost instantly when Marco had introduced her to us.

"Well," I said while briefly sinking my teeth into my bottom lip. "We're hoping to have kids sooner rather than later."

"I'm so glad you have each other," she said before Marco spun her.

And a parade of the past gathered in my mind as I stared into the eyes of my husband. From the moment I first met Adam back at Les' flat . . . to when I'd learned he was a fighter.

And then a dozen more memories after that—all leading me to tonight . . . to our happily-ever-after.

CHAPTER NINETEEN

ANNA

"You went running on the beach? Alone?" Adam strode toward me in faded blue jeans, the top button not fastened as I polished off my water.

"I couldn't resist. This place is gorgeous. Besides, you were sleeping, and I didn't want to wake you." I tossed the bottle in the recycling before he hopped onto the kitchen counter in our villa in Bora Bora. "We're on our honeymoon, by the way. You don't need to worry about me." I stepped in front of him and placed my palms on each side of the counter, and his gaze dropped down to my sports bra.

"Sorry, love, I'll always worry about you." He shrugged. "And how many blokes hit on you while you were out there?" He cocked his head, his denim-blue eyes narrowing when he looked at my face again.

I lifted one shoulder. "Three. Maybe four," I joked.

"Mm. Maybe I didn't get you a big enough ring to ward them off." His lips teased into a smile as he reached for my hand and eyed my ring finger.

"And you know I don't care for flashy things." I didn't need some fancy mega-diamond to weigh my hand down either. I stepped back, and he released my hand, and my tongue pinned to the roof of my mouth as I took in the sight of my sexy husband.

My casual and carefree man.

I'd never seen him so at ease since I'd known him.

Seven days on vacation, and we had two more.

"You want to go snorkeling today?" He hopped off the counter and braced his hands on my hips.

"The idea of being underwater and . . ." I shook my head. "I just don't know if I can do it."

"And I'd never pressure you, but sometimes doing what we're afraid of can be the most rewarding." He pressed a quick kiss to my lips. "Look at me. Falling in love scared the bloody hell out of me, and yet here I am with you, and I couldn't be happier."

I'd once thought this man would crush my heart. That he'd destroy me. And instead, he brought me to life.

"Maybe. If we're in the clearest part of the water, and it's not too deep." My thoughts buzzed to memories of watching *Jaws* with my sisters when we were kids.

Yeah, not a fan of sharks.

Nope.

"On second thought—"

"How about you join me in bed?"

I looked down at my sweat-covered body. "Maybe a shower first?"

He reached between our bodies and tugged my running shorts and panties down to my mid-thighs. He rubbed at the achiness between my legs, and I shuddered, leaning into his touch.

"Always ready for me, huh?" He nipped my earlobe as he continued to drive me crazy with only his hand.

I pulled away and peeled off my sticky sports bra to free my breasts.

A chill blew up my back despite the heat pouring in through the open windows.

"These tits," he said while palming one, maintaining his fingers at my wet center with his other hand. "Perfect," he said in a throaty voice.

"Shower or sex?" I tipped my chin and looked skyward as I resisted coming right there. I braced my hands on his sides and rotated my hips, and my shorts fell to my ankles at the movement.

"How about both?" He sucked at the sensitive part of my neck beneath my earlobe. "And how about we never leave this place?"

ADAM

I buried my face between her legs, and she grabbed at my head, holding me in place as I went down on her.

She growled out, "I'm gonna come too soon. Not yet."

Her words only had me itching to make her come even more. I kissed her inner thighs before finding her soaked center again then placed two fingers inside of her.

"Okay," she whispered. "Maybe don't . . . stop."

Her body began to quiver beneath me as she orgasmed, and then I trailed my lips up her abdomen before sucking at a puckered pink nipple.

"I need you inside of me," she pleaded, her voice straining, as she lifted her body off the bed to get closer.

"As you wish, my love." I found her mouth and slipped

my tongue between her parted lips, then positioned my tip at her center and dove into her in one fast movement.

"Adam," she cried as I moved in time with her.

I'd lost count of how many times we'd made love on our honeymoon, and wasn't that the way it was supposed to be?

I flicked my tongue with hers, my balls tightening, the blood rushing through my body—my dick hardening to the point of fecking pain.

If I didn't blow my load soon, I'd lose my damn mind.

I wasn't some sixty-second man, but the idea I could get her pregnant right now had everything inside of me igniting to an all-new level.

"Anna," I murmured after she came again, and only then did I allow myself to release before falling off to the side of her.

She lifted her knees to her chest.

"What are you doing?" I rolled to my side and propped my head up with my hand to better view her.

"Trying to keep your sperm inside me. Maybe we'll get lucky on our first attempt." She looked over at me, a smile in her eyes.

"My guys are fighters," I said with a laugh, and my words had her cheeks lifting with a broad smile. "But to be on the safe side, we should do this about fifty more times before we leave this island."

She lowered her legs. "Fifty?" She chuckled. "We leave in two days."

"I extended our trip. One more week."

"What?" Her mouth opened in shock, and she moved to her side and pressed a palm flat to my chest.

My eyes lingered on the swell of her breasts as she took in a deep breath, and then my attention traveled to her pouty mouth. “We still haven’t gone snorkeling, and I was hoping maybe you’d change your mind.”

“You’re so persistent.” She bit into her bottom lip, her eyes lifting as if in thought.

“I got you, didn’t I? Winning your heart wasn’t the easiest of feats.”

“Like you said . . . you’re a fighter. No way would you give up without getting me.”

“Mm. And I’ll never give up on you.” I slanted my lips over hers to steal a quick kiss. “Never give up on *us*. And I’ll always lay everything on the line to keep you safe. To keep you happy.”

She touched her forehead to mine and whispered, “Ditto.”

EPILOGUE

ANNA

"I'm gonna go bloody nuts waiting. Are you sure it hasn't been two minutes yet?"

I fidgeted with the hem of my black tee and stared at the closed bathroom door. "I'm not ready to look."

He reached for my hand and held it tight. "We'll never know if we don't open that door."

"What if it's negative?" My pulse raced, my palms grew sweaty.

"Then we keep trying. And the trying part is pretty damn fun if you ask me." He pulled me into his arms and kissed me.

We were finally at the home we built in Dublin, and it'd been three weeks since we left Bora Bora, and well, my period was three days late.

That was a good sign, but what if . . .

"If it's negative you promise we start trying again? I mean, I doubt I'm ovulating," I said with a smile, "but practice makes perfect."

"Yeah, and I think we'll need to practice a few times a day. What do you think?"

"Maybe we start right this second?" I stepped back and peeled off my black tee and flung it.

His eyes dropped to my breasts, but he lifted his hands in the air between us. "Nice try, but you can't distract me with sex." He looked back over his shoulder at the en suite bathroom door. "First, we get the results. And then after, regardless, we make love."

"Fine." I grabbed my T-shirt and slipped it back over my head.

He took hold of my hand and guided me toward the bathroom, my heartbeat skipping a few beats in the process.

Once the door was open, I pressed my free hand over my eyes, too nervous. "You look first."

"No." He reached for my wrist and lowered my arm to my side. "We do this together." His thumb swept a small circle over my cheek, and he leaned in to plant another kiss on my lips. "Whatever happens, it's what's meant to be. Okay?"

I swallowed my nerves and nodded. "You're right."

We both took a calming breath and went over to the pregnancy stick atop the vanity counter, but I snapped my eyes closed before I could see whether there were one or two pink lines.

"Two lines means you and . . . a baby?"

My stomach dropped.

"Is that what you see?" I opened one eye and forced myself to look at his palm.

Two pink lines. Two very dark pink lines.

"Oh my God." I stepped back and covered my mouth.

"Told you my boys are fighters." Tears welled in his eyes as he stared at me.

"We're pregnant?" I whispered and brought my hand to

my abdomen as if I'd feel my first kick already. "Is there really a part of you inside of me?"

He set the stick down and placed his palm over my heart. "I'd like to think I'm already here," he said in a low voice as a tear hit his cheek, and I could feel the tears from my eyes falling as well. "But yes, my love, you've got my child in ya now."

I looped my arms around my husband, never wanting to let go. "I'm so happy. Thank you."

"Imagine your happiness and multiply it by a thousand—that's what I'm feeling." His brows knitted, and his voice broke. "Thank you for coming to Dublin. Thank you for trusting me with your heart." His Irish brogue traveled through his speech more prominently than normal, which usually happened when he became emotional.

"I wouldn't trust it with anyone else," I whispered and leaned into his embrace for a kiss.

Dublin Nights continues with Holly & Sebastian in *THE REAL DEAL*. Continue to learn more about other characters from *On the Line*.

Made in the USA
Coppell, TX
28 September 2023